VILLA PARAISO

VILLA PARAISO

A Novel

LEE B. RAVINE

Library of Congress Cataloging-in-Publication Data

Ravine, Lee B.
Villa Paraiso: A Novel

p. cm.
Paperback ISBN: 978-1-947708-16-7
Ebook ISBN: 978-1-947708-17-4
Library of Congress Control Number: 2018947563

10 9 8 7 6 5 4 3 2 1
First Edition, July 2018

CITRINE PUBLISHING
Fort Lauderdale, Florida, U.S.A.
(561) 299-1150
Publisher@CitrinePublishing.com
www.CitrinePublishing.com

Also by Lee B. Ravine

_____

Riding Solo My Journey Through Love and Madness

*This book is dedicated to the memory of
Sylvia Altman, Henri Borstel and
Estelle O'Polyn*

ONE

A GENTLE TROPICAL BREEZE carried jasmine's sweet scent across Villa Paraiso's serene landscape as an owl's high-pitched screech pierced the silence.

Hector detected movement in the murky predawn darkness. He scuttled across the damp grass until he reached a narrow opening in the neatly manicured hedge. His eyes darted back and forth in search of a nocturnal creature or stray pet. He wiped his sweaty palms across the front of his shirt.

A lone parked car rocked to a silent beat, slowly at first, until it settled into a steady *dadum dadum dadum*.

Hector crept closer. Pounding blood surged through his veins.

The car doors opened and slammed shut, followed by the sound of passionate kisses and soulful moans.

Hector strained to hear the couple's conversation. He didn't recognize the woman's voice, but her companion sounded like Charles, Villa Paraiso's dance instructor.

"Tomorrow?" the man asked.

"Uh-uh. Not tomorrow."

"Then when? You know how disappointed I am when I don't see you."

"Please don't pressure me. I love to be with you too, but I can't be pinned down to a specific day."

The couple kissed before Hector heard the sound of sneakers kicking up gravel, as the woman bounded across the parking lot.

The man spit on the ground. "Boca bitch." He entered his car and sped away.

Hector stood and brushed off blades of grass as dawn's first light appeared over the horizon. He hurried off in the direction of the corrugated metal maintenance shed nicknamed The Equator.

TWO

BURT ROSEN HAD BEEN a conservative investor. He believed slow and steady wins the race. He and his wife Sharon had lived modestly and worked hard to build a successful accounting practice in New Jersey. She never complained, not even during the time Burt studied for his CPA exam and she had to assume more responsibility, both at work and at home. She focused on their ultimate goal, that one day they'd retire to Florida.

On dreary winter mornings Sharon would twirl around their bedroom in her flannel nightgown and fuzzy slippers. "I can see myself now. I'm wearing Gucci sunglasses and a huge floppy hat." She'd spread her arms to indicate spectacular proportions. "I'm sitting in a café overlooking the ocean. A balmy breeze teases the folds of my sundress as I sip margaritas and nibble delectable wedges of quesadilla."

As a result of Burt's financial acumen, he and Sharon had put two sons through college and contributed to the down payment on their homes. But in recent years business had fallen off due to competition from nationwide accounting firms and income tax preparation software.

After years of planning, Burt found himself faced with the unpleasant task of informing Sharon that the extravagant retirement lifestyle she had envisioned was out of the question.

After he awoke from a restless night dreaming about wild dogs chasing him through a dense forest, he couldn't put off telling Sharon about their dismal finances any longer. He retrieved the spreadsheets from the den and flicked on the light over the chrome-trimmed, Formica kitchen table. He placed the reports on the smooth surface and waited.

Sharon entered the kitchen a short time later. She kissed Burt on top of his head and proceeded to dig into the coffee canister with a measuring spoon. "There, that's done," she said, after she counted out the desired amount of coffee, filled the coffee-maker's reservoir with tap water and pushed the "on" button.

She turned back around and was shocked to see Burt's pale face. "What's wrong? You don't look well, you need some water." She reached for a glass.

"Forget the damn water. Sit down."

The urgency in his tone alarmed Sharon. She turned off the faucet and sat down at the table.

"This isn't going to be easy," Burt said. "I've always taken pride in my thoroughness. I've worked hard… we both have, but things haven't turned out the way I'd hoped. We… I… fell short of our retirement goal."

"Just how bad is it?"

Silence.

"Burt. Answer me."

"Let's just say, it's not good."

Burt stared into Sharon's eyes hoping to see absolution. What he found was a face set in stone and a fiery glare that threatened to ignite the pages spread across the table.

"No!" Sharon shrieked and repeatedly slapped her temples. "No, no, no, no, no!"

Burt rose to his feet and tried to grab her hands, but she pushed him away.

"Sharon, I'm only saying that we have to move the target date back a little and if we buy something less expensive—"

"I don't believe what I'm hearing. There must be some mistake. Tell me you mixed up our financial report with a client's. Tell me I'm crazy or I'm hallucinating. No, tell me you're crazy. Yes, that's it. I'm living with a crazy man."

"You have every right to be upset. It's not what either of us expected. I'm sorry."

Sharon bowed her head and cried softly at first. Her sobs grew louder, before escalating to hysterical laughter. Her tirade ended as suddenly as it began. She pushed her chair back and lost her footing, fell forward, and struck her head on the edge of the table. Her knees buckled.

Burt grabbed a dish towel and filled it with ice cubes. He knelt beside her and placed the ice pack over her bloody wound.

Sharon pulled the towel from his hand and flung it across the kitchen. Ice cubes flew in all directions. "A doctor, now you're a doctor? You screwed up as an accountant and now you're a doctor." Despite her trembling hands she managed to pull herself upright and stumble out of the room.

Burt crumpled the meticulously prepared spreadsheets and tossed them in with the trash. He sat back down at the table feeling like a murderer awaiting the jury's verdict.

He started to worry about Sharon's long absence, and was just about to check on her, when she returned to the kitchen with a gauze bandage affixed to her forehead.

She glared at Burt, hands on hips, legs splayed. "I deserve the prize that was promised when I signed on for this life," she said. "I want the goddamned condo in Florida and no amount of whining or lame excuses will change that. Do you hear me? I don't care if you have to beg, borrow, or steal. We're moving to Florida."

* * *

Burt and Sharon rarely deviated from their new morning routine. Up before dawn, they drank coffee in silence, seated across from each other on uncomfortable wrought iron chairs. The bistro set had been featured in a home decorating magazine. Sharon insisted it was the "in" thing, an absolute must-have for casual dining. She had made a convincing argument. "A full-size table with four chairs is *passé*. After all, it's just for the two of us. You know, for breakfast or a quick cup of coffee and a sandwich."

Burt enjoyed reading the newspaper first thing in the morning, but there was barely enough room on the little table to lay it flat. "You never should have bought this set."

"Really, *I* shouldn't have bought it?"

"Sure, I drove you to the store, I handed the salesman my credit card, but you had already made up your mind to buy this… this…"

"Bistro set, Burt. It's called a *bistro set*. It looks great, it fits perfectly in here. What's wrong with it?"

"I hate this damn table, it's too small." *God forbid we should eat in the dining room on the overpriced floor sample purchased at a decorator's clearance sale chairs not included.*

Sharon had forbidden him to use the elegant, glass-topped table reserved for neighbors she hoped to entertain in the future.

Burt eventually found the courage to speak up. "It takes time to cultivate friendships in a new community. In the meantime, we're not enjoying our dining room."

Sharon frowned. "Do you have any idea what a job it is to keep the table clean? Even if we eat on one end, I have to remove the silk floral arrangement and spray the entire table with Windex. If I have to do it every day I'm worried I'll scratch the glass. And I have to vacuum the area rug underneath after we've finished eating, and besides," they completed the sentence in unison, "the dining room is for company."

Burt rinsed his cup and put it in the dishwasher, as per Sharon's retirement rules. He entered the master bedroom and pulled on the walking shorts and T-shirt he'd tossed onto a chair instead of on the floor the previous day—another one of Sharon's retirement rules—and walked past her headed toward the front door.

"Burt, where are you going? It's still dark outside."

He didn't dare say one word, certain that if he responded, this would surely be their last day together. He disliked everything about his new life, Sharon most of all.

Burt wandered aimlessly and was about to step onto a narrow gravel path when from behind, the sound of screeching brakes stopped him in his tracks. He turned in time to see a man sprint across the road and disappear from view.

Burt wondered if the man was running away from his wife, too, and suddenly felt ridiculous. "What the hell am I doing out here?"

He headed back to the villa just as a fiery glow pierced the horizon. *Today is gonna be a scorcher,* he thought, but couldn't care less. He was more concerned with surviving retirement and spending twenty-four hours a day with Sharon.

THREE

EACH MORNING, EMILY BAYER awoke to the empty bed she had shared with her beloved husband Harry. She let out a sigh filled with resignation and lovingly patted his undisturbed pillow.

Harry had experienced a fatal heart attack six months after they had moved to Villa Paraiso. Up until that fateful day the couple had been inseparable. Remembering those times brought a smile to Emily's lips.

"What do you feel like doing today, Harry?"

"Hmm, let's see. I'd like you to give me a full-body massage and in lieu of lunch, read aloud from that erotic novel everybody's talking about while feeding me peeled grapes."

"And then?"

"The answer is obvious. Either I'll chase you around the house until we both fall over from exhaustion, or we climb into bed and take a nap."

"Know what?"

"Yup... I'm the best."

"That's true, Harry, but if you drive me to Festival Flea Market, you'll be the greatest!"

The screened patio offered relief from mosquitoes, but little else. Despite the heat and humidity Emily reclined on a chaise lounge, sipped a steaming hot cup of chamomile tea, and waited for the sun to appear. She savored the early morning quiet before residents began their daily routines. Several women she'd met occupied their days shopping, gossiping over lunch, visiting the spa, or participating in their dermatologist's "Cosmetic Day," code name for the procedure *du jour*: Botox, Restylane, or Juvéderm. She had no desire to get caught up in the minutiae.

Emily was startled by a rustling sound near the hedge that separated her villa from the lake. She hoped it was her imagination run amok, or a raccoon, or even one of those ghastly reptiles, anything but a burglar. She clutched her nightgown to her neck in an attempt at modesty, just in case.

A shadowy figure emerged from behind a shrub, and moved closer. Emily jumped up off the lounge. Her cup bounced on the imported Italian tiles she and Harry had painstakingly chosen together. On the last bounce the cup shattered and scattered pieces of crockery across the floor.

By the time she looked up, the prowler had moved out of her field of vision. She considered dialing 9-1-1 or alerting security, but she was afraid they'd accuse her of sounding like a foolish old woman imagining things that go *bump* in the night.

She stared at the remains of her favorite cup and sobbed, "Harry, why… why did you leave me?"

FOUR

PEGGY BELL AND HER SON ROGER were a source of curiosity and speculation, fodder for the gossip mill, an integral part of life in a gated community.

She found it amusing that a few of the residents assumed she was a sixty-something cougar cohabitating with her cub.

Back in Boston, Peggy had defended her son to tongue-clucking family and friends. Holiday gatherings had been particularly unsettling. Her sister never missed an opportunity to prattle about what she referred to as Roger's "sensitive side."

"You're blowing things out of proportion," Peggy had said one Easter Sunday, deviled eggs sliding precariously toward the edge of the serving platter held in her outstretched hands.

"I know a *namby-pamby* when I see one," Aunt Millie chirped. "What sort of man works in a... a tearoom?"

"Roger's your favorite nephew. How can you say something that outrageous? And you know darn well that he *owns* the tearoom at the antique mall."

Aunt Millie curled her lips into a sardonic smile. "He's still my favorite nephew, he's fruity is all I'm saying." She grabbed a deviled egg and stuffed it into her mouth.

During a long, brutal winter and after much discussion, Roger and his mother decided to sell their home and the tearoom, and relocate to a warmer climate. In the past couple of years his business had declined, while at the same time his mother's painful arthritic knees had become unbearable.

* * *

After they settled into their new home, to show his appreciation for the times his mother had defended him in the past, Roger acted as her escort. One night each week he was free to pursue whatever made *him* happy. He accepted the arrangement without complaint, anxious to avoid being labeled a "pathetic slut" by his gay peers.

However, the same scenario ensued each time he was on his way out for the evening.

"Roger dear, *must* you go out tonight?"

"Mother, you do remember our arrangement?"

"Of course I do, but I just thought—"

He placed his finger across her lips and kissed her forehead before heading out the door.

Peggy had given up hope that her only child would settle down with a lovely young woman and make her a proud grandma. All she wished for now was for Roger to find happiness. But no matter how hard she tried to make sense of her son's lifestyle, she never understood the allure of same-sex liaisons. The thought of sweaty, inebriated men groping each other, hoping to culminate their evening with an anonymous sexual encounter, repulsed her. She found it difficult to accept that *her* son participated in such repugnant activities. She and her pastor back home had devoted countless hours to praying the gay away, but to no avail.

Roger had never felt comfortable with the hookups and promiscuity that was so much a part of the gay lifestyle. After he'd met a couple of creeps on Grindr he was convinced it was safer to pursue a relationship face-to-face from the get-go.

Blush, the popular late-night melting pot for gays, bisexuals, transgenders, and the undecided, was located in a former warehouse off of I-95. The club offered a respite from prying eyes. Late at night, there was rarely anyone in the secluded industrial park to ponder the comings and goings of the diverse and often flamboyant clientele.

On this particular night, Roger noticed an unusual number of new faces and gay-for-pay party boys, a result of the International LGBTQ conference at the nearby convention center.

When it came to hooking-up with an unknown quantity, he had developed a sixth sense—a sort of "gaydar." He had experienced one incident in which he had misjudged and ended up with a surprise package missing a crucial piece of equipment.

Most of the homosexuals he encountered were up-front about their sexual predilection, while bisexuals tended to be divisive and deflect AC/DC inquiries. He found trannies brash and exaggerated in their effort to convince the interested party that they're as genuine on the outside as they are on the inside. Curious wannabes were a whole different story. They'd attempt to hide their nervousness with a false bravado, while perspiring profusely or avoiding eye contact.

By 4 a.m., the enthusiastic crowd that had grinded and groped their way through much of the night had thinned out. The interviewing process Roger used to determine whether a particular candidate was either fish or fowl proved to be a tedious bore. He'd lost interest in making small talk, slow dancing to throbbing electronic music and maintaining the level of intensity necessary for a "happy ending." He had had enough socializing for one night and wasn't looking forward to the long drive home.

The sticker affixed to Roger's car window allowed him to access Villa Paraiso's electronic entry system without rousing the dozing guard. He hadn't driven more than twenty yards, before a figure dressed in dark clothing, with a cap pulled down low on his head, darted in front of his car. Startled, Roger slammed on the brakes. He shook his head. *With all the alcohol I drank we're both lucky I didn't kill the sonofabitch.*

Desperate to throw himself into bed before his mother awakened, Roger focused his attention on navigating the road leading to their villa.

FIVE

HECTOR ENTERED the maintenance shed's vacant washroom and steadied himself against the sink. Perspiration matted his chest hair. His armpits emitted a rank odor, a combination of spices, grease, and beer. He blotted his torso with paper towels.

He considered confiding in his friend Manny about almost being run over, but then he'd have to explain why he was sneaking around before daybreak.

A chance meeting with Manny at a local sports bar had led to a sleeping room in a house shared with three strangers, an introduction to Manny's boss and a job at Villa Paraiso, no questions asked.

Manny had often boasted about the love-starved women he'd serviced and offered to introduce Hector to a *puta* looking for a poke in her *piñata*. Hector found the idea offensive. He respected women and preferred to worship them from afar. He avoided intimacy, all the while tormented by his aberration.

Farley, Villa Paraiso's maintenance supervisor, was seated on a high stool behind a makeshift podium. He towered over the captive audience huddled around him. Broken blood vessels mottled his ruddy complexion, the result of years of alcohol abuse.

The smug look on his face reflected his superior attitude toward what he considered the wasteland of humanity standing before him. The arrogant redneck had zero tolerance for the crude immigrants he supervised and never missed an opportunity to remind them his daddy had been a preacher. "When I was a boy, back in *Ma-con-jo-ja*, my daddy useta say, 'I'd sooner lynch the likes of y'all than look y'all in the eye'."

The maintenance workers despised the pot-bellied Anglo with the fiery red hair and crooked yellow teeth. On sweltering hot days if Farley had it in for a particular employee, the merciless bastard would give the subject of his disdain the most arduous assignment. Overworked, underpaid and far from home and loved ones, more than a few of them would have loved to see him dead.

During their lunch breaks, the men gathered in small groups wherever they found a patch of shade and discussed numerous ways to kill the pink-skinned pig. The possibilities seemed endless. Weigh him down with rocks and toss him into a canal, drop him into a barrel of lye and watch him dissolve, tie him up and drive him out to Alligator Alley and let the gators finish him off.

Despite his coworkers' enthusiasm, Hector refused to get involved in their gruesome schemes. He preferred to keep to himself, often deep in thought as he struggled to understand the invisible force that robbed him of his free will.

Hector sat on his haunches a few yards from the other men. He blotted beads of sweat with the outside of his lunch bag before he removed the contents and tore into his sandwich.

Eduardo moved closer, his lips curled in an ugly sneer. "You too good for us man?"

Hector ignored him and continued to eat his boring *queso blanco* sandwich.

Eduardo's coal black mustache danced under a nose covered with angry red pustules. He leaned over and jabbed Hector's chest with his index finger. "I ask you somethin' man, why you no answer?"

Flecks of spittle bounced off Hector's cheek. He imagined a wild dog ready to attack. "Look, Eduardo... I ain' botherin' nobody. Let me be."

Eduardo yanked Hector to his feet. "You sittin' off by yourself. Don' never talk to nobody. You doin' your own schemin' and shit and don' wan' us to know nothin'?"

"Yeah," several of the men chimed in. "He up to no good."

"I no lookin' for trouble. Jus' wanna eat my stinkin' cheese sandwich."

Manny interrupted, "Come on guys, cool it. Besides, lunch break's almost over."

Hector stuffed what was left of the sandwich into his mouth, shoved the crumpled bag into his pocket, and returned to his utility cart.

His work order was attached to a plot-map that indicated the location of the vast sprinkler system. Red "X's" marked the malfunctioning units listed on the accompanying service requests. He placed his clipboard on the seat beside him and filled a plastic cup from the cooler. He took a few sips of the funky water and poured what was left onto the ground.

Hector's cart bumped along pedestrian paths and traversed lush green lawns. He reflected on life before he arrived in the Sunshine State. He recalled how his three older brothers stumbled through life in an alcoholic stupor and eventually ended up dead or in jail. He imagined he was a *niño* on his way home from school. His *mamacita,* a saint who had rubbed her fingers raw scrubbing coarse garments and cooking scant meals with the meager salary his father earned as a farm worker, waved from the doorway. Shortly after his mother fell ill, his father left for work one morning and never returned home, unwilling to care for the woman who no longer fulfilled his sexual demands. Several months later, after his mother died, Hector packed a duffle bag and snuck over the Mexican border in the dead of night.

Hector's thoughts were interrupted by a loud "thump." He hopped off the cart to assess the situation and discovered a palm frond wedged between the front axle and the undercarriage. He reached for his tool belt and cursed under his breath, "'Nother fuckin' day in paradise."

SIX

TWO YEARS EARLIER, at an all-night poker game, Peter Duke learned that the forty-something player seated opposite him, nervously licking his lips, planned to develop a gated, residential community in Boca Raton, Florida. Despite the recent downturn in the economy and a record-breaking number of foreclosures and defaults on construction loans, the man sounded optimistic.

Peter doubted the man's credibility, but decided to run the information by his old buddy, Stu Campbell. Their history went way back. Friends since grade school, they had double-dated with their then-future wives, now ex-wives, and were best man at each other's weddings.

Stu settled in Miami, renovated depressed houses in foreclosure and flipped them for a handsome profit. It wasn't long before he expanded his real estate business to include luxury properties.

Peter remained in New York and enjoyed a modest degree of success managing housing developments throughout the five boroughs and acquired smaller properties at auction. He liked to think of himself as an entrepreneur.

It had been quite some time since Peter had touched base with Stu.

"Hey Stu, it's me, Peter. How the hell are you?"

"Same old, same old. What's up with you?"

"I'm good... great, in fact. Listen, I'm calling because I heard something interesting during a poker game the other night. Personally, I think the information's a load of crap, but I'd like to run it by you and hear what you think."

"I'm listening."

"Well, the guys are bullshitting, you know the usual, who banged what, where and for how long."

Stu sounded preoccupied. "Uh-huh. Uh-huh."

"Hope I haven't interrupted anything important."

"No, no. Go ahead. I'm all ears."

"This asshole tells us that instead of wasting our time wearing out our little heads, we should be using our big heads to make some real moola. This guy Louis bragged about inheriting a shitload of property along with a produce packing and distributing business. His grandfather was a savvy businessman back in the 1920s. The old guy purchased Boca farmland for eight hundred dollars an acre. Calculating the appreciation on that investment makes my head spin."

"Tell me more."

"Anyhow, the longer he talked, the more certain I was that if he was telling the truth about developing a gated community, he doesn't have what it takes to handle a project that size on his own. He didn't strike me as a businessman. The way I see it, if we get involved and pick up a piece of the action, we stand to make a nice profit."

"You make it sound too easy."

"You're slowing down Stu, lost your edge. Must be too many hotties sapping your energy."

"I wish. Look, Peter, new construction can take years before it's approved by the county planning and zoning commission and state and federal regulatory agencies."

"The wheels have already been set in motion," Peter said.

The project's been approved. We can jump right on this. Somebody's going to take advantage of this greenhorn, why not us?"

"Sounds good, but we're dealing with a new generation of home buyers. Country Clubs don't fit the baby boomer lifestyle. They don't share their grandfathers' idea of retirement. They'd rather use the old noodle than drag their asses around a golf course. And as for early-bird dinners, they're certainly not willing to wear jackets in the clubhouse past six o'clock to eat a hamburger. And there's one more thing."

"What's that?"

"I'm not used to dealing with middle-class, bourgeois, Jewish clientele. My expertise is in relocating retired corporate executives to multi-million dollar properties with deep-water access."

"Let me put your mind at ease, Stu. First off, the community's master plan doesn't include a golf course. Second, this Louis plans to modify clubhouse regulations with an emphasis on casual dress. And as far as the clientele, he assured me that Boca's changed. It's no longer predominately Jewish. Churches and synagogues are right next to each other."

"Based on what you've told me—your words—'this asshole,' I'm a little hesitant to get involved."

"I might have exaggerated, but the project deserves a closer look."

"All right, you've sold me."

"It's settled then, you're in?"

"Yup, and you'd make a great director of operations, collecting kick-backs and chasing secretaries around the boardroom."

Peter cleared his scratchy throat, a reminder of too many late nights in smoke-filled card rooms. "From your mouth…"

"How do we get in touch with this Louis?"

"I have his contact information in front of me."

"Call him and arrange a meeting for the three of us in Atlantic City. I figure one day should do it, two at most."

"I knew I could count on you Stu, but why A.C.?"

"I can kill two birds with one stone. I don't often have the opportunity to visit my youngest daughter. She's in a graduate program at N.Y.U. I plan to spend a few days with her in Manhattan."

"You're one lucky guy. My kids barely speak to me."

"Sorry to hear that."

"Yeah… yeah, that's the way it goes sometimes. I'll get on this as soon as I hang up."

"Sounds like a plan."

SEVEN

PETER'S STOREFRONT OFFICE was where he hung his hat when he wasn't playing poker or harassing tenants in one of his rundown tenements.

The drab surroundings consisted of two metal desks, a well-worn faux leather couch, four folding chairs, and a scarred oak desk and a swivel chair from a bygone era. Metal file cabinets lined one wall and overgrown pots of jade plants monopolized the space beneath the plate glass window.

Peter relished Sundays alone in his sanctuary. He ignored the blinking light on the answering machine. Complaints would wait until his sister Jeanne opened the office Monday morning. He tugged at the file drawer where he'd stashed a bottle of Jack Daniel's, but the drawer wouldn't budge. He cursed under his breath and shook the warped drawer with both hands until it slid open just enough to allow him to retrieve the bottle.

He poured two fingers of Scotch into a smudged drinking glass and carried his drink to the front window, partially obstructed by the peeling "Real Estate Management" sign. He gazed out at a piss-yellow patch of snow and took a sip of the smooth amber liquid.

His thoughts drifted back to the year his father had skipped out on the family. His mother worked double shifts at a local diner in order to support him and his younger sister. Late one night, his mother had stumbled into the house, her face bruised and her auburn hair matted with blood.

He'd leapt from the armchair in front of the TV. "What the hell happened to you?" he'd said.

"I'll be all right," she'd answered. "Just help me lie down."

He lowered his mother onto the threadbare sofa. Tufts of cotton batting circled her head like a halo.

Alarmed by her limp body he cried out, "Ma... *ma!*"

Her eyelids fluttered. She held out her hand.

Peter helped her sit up. "Ma, tell me what happened."

"Some bastard mugged me. He stole my tips, my pay-check, everything."

"Why did he have to beat you up? Why? He got what he wanted."

"I held onto my purse and screamed, but no one heard me. He kept punching me until I let go." She touched her bruised cheek and winced. "He ran off and I stumbled back into the diner."

Peter clenched his fists.

His mother wagged her finger. "Don't do nothin' crazy. I'd never survive if something happened to you."

Up until that moment, Peter hadn't realized how much she'd sacrificed for him and his sister. "Someday you'll have the life you deserve, Ma, I promise."

The ringing phone interrupted his thoughts. He listened as the answering machine picked up.

"What's wrong with you people?" Have a little *rach-munus,* a little pity for your tenants. Again, the elevator is broken. How many times—" The machine beeped before it cut off. The message box was full.

Mrs. Ehrlich, he thought. *Damn that woman. One of these days I'm going to put the fear of God into her.*

EIGHT

BRIGHT AND EARLY Monday morning, Peter dialed Louis' cell number. The call went directly to voice mail. He waited two hours before he tried the number again. This time Louis answered after the fourth ring.

"Hello! Hello!" Louis said.

"It's Peter Duke."

"Who?"

"Peter Duke. We met at a poker—"

"Oh yeah, I remember now. What's up?"

"Well, my partner Stu and I are interested in getting involved in your project. We'd like to arrange a face-to-face and kick around a few ideas with you. Then, if all parties are in agreement—"

"I… I don't know. I feel uneasy involving strangers in my business."

"With millions of dollars at stake, I can understand your concern. There's an awful lot to deal with here, way too much for one person to handle without help. You'll need experienced people you can count on to deal with contractors and staff, and the problems that are bound to arise in a project this size."

Not getting a response, Peter continued, "If you'll

consider working with a management team I'd like to propose myself and my business associate, Stu Campbell, to head up that team."

"I don't appreciate having strangers breathing down my neck and scrutinizing my every move."

"That's exactly why you need a project manager so you won't have to deal with everything yourself."

"I might've taken on more than I can handle. Right now I've got a migraine that just won't quit. I'm not sure who to trust, or what I should do."

What's with this guy? He's all over the map, Peter thought, but greed clouded his judgment. "At least consider my offer. You'll be making a huge mistake if you pass it up."

By the end of the phone conversation, Louis had reluctantly agreed to meet with Peter and Stu in Atlantic City the following week.

* * *

In fact, the Boca project had come up at a perfect time. Peter was tired of the same old, same old. In his mid-fifties and divorced twice, he was open to exploring new options. During his absence, he'd rely on his sister to handle the mail and make bank deposits. His burly nephew, Ralphie, would handle delinquent rent collections and deal with tenants' complaints. If there were any major problems that required his personal attention, he'd fly up for a few days.

Lulled by the hissing radiator, Peter's eyelids drooped and he drifted off to sleep. In his dream, he was a young stud. Bikini-clad nymphs were toasting him with crystal flutes filled with champagne and beckoning from a bubbling Jacuzzi surrounded by palm trees.

NINE

PETER HAD MANAGED TO FINAGLE a spacious comp at the Golden Chariot Hotel and Casino. He had hoped that sharing the three-bedroom suite would allow him to observe his potential business associate up close and personal, before he and Stu made a commitment.

Peter arrived early and poured himself a drink from the well-stocked bar. He sank into a luxuriously upholstered sofa and was just beginning to relax. He was startled when the suite's double doors flew open and Louis lurched into the sitting room.

He resembled a grinning marionette with his head bobbing and limbs flailing. He dropped his overnight bag and kicked the doors closed.

"Great room, awesome view, TV gotta be seventy inches at least."

For a moment, Peter was speechless.

Louis lunged for the remote control and flipped through the channels. "Look at that reception. It's like I'm in there, man! Reminds me of when I dropped acid in college." He clicked off the TV, hopped onto a barstool and acknowledged Peter. "Good to see you." He tossed the remote in the air, tried to catch it and missed.

"Yeah, yeah, good to see you, too," Peter said half-heartedly. He bent down and retrieved the remote that had skittered off the glass coffee table.

The phone rang.

This had better be Stu.

It was.

"I'll be a little late," Stu said. "Limo's stuck in rush hour traffic."

Peter rolled his eyes. "No problem. I've got it all under control. See you soon." *I hope.*

Louis paced back and forth. "I knew it. I knew something would go wrong. Didn't sleep a wink last night, had an uneasy feeling about this meeting and now your partner's— what— not coming?"

"Relax. Stu's just running a little late. Traffic's a bitch at this hour." *Where's the happy puppet from two minutes ago?* Peter stepped in back of the bar and reached for the bottle of Glenlivet's single malt whiskey. "You need to unwind with a good stiff drink and I'm just the guy who can pour one."

Louis gasped, "Can't breathe, need air." He staggered to the double-doors, pulled them open and raced down the corridor.

Peter chased after him.

Louis stopped in front of an elevator and repeatedly pushed the "down" button. The floor indicator light moved from fifteen to sixteen. He looked around frantically. "Where's the fire exit?"

"We're on the twenty-third floor."

"I can't wait any longer!"

The elevator doors slid open.

Louis froze in place

Peter shoved him forward. *What the hell have I gotten myself into? Guy's a nutcase.*

The elevator went straight to the casino floor. Louis bolted the moment the doors opened. He headed for the nearest exit and almost collided with a cocktail waitress balancing a serving tray filled with empty glasses.

Peter raced through the hotel lobby and out onto the street where he found Louis clinging to a wall with one hand and clutching his chest with the other. "Jesus, Louis, you're scaring me."

"I know, I know. I'm sorry, man."

"Are you okay?"

"Yeah, just give me a minute."

"Do you have these episodes often?"

No response.

Peter guided Louis back inside to the lobby lounge. A perky cocktail waitress took their drink order. While they waited for their drinks, Peter watched Louis fold and unfold a cocktail napkin in a series of Origami configurations. He marveled at Louis' dexterity despite his compromised mental state. "I couldn't do that if my life depended on it."

"My shrink suggested I keep my hands busy. It helps me relax and avoid these… panic attacks."

Peter chose to ignore the remark and instead directed Louis' attention to the disheveled young man seated at the bar. "See that guy over there ogling the broads?"

"Yeah, so what?"

"The guy has balls. He's trying to pick up broads looking like a slob."

"Maybe he has issues."

"No shit."

Louis lowered his voice. "There was a time in my life when I slid into a deep depression. I didn't shower for days and slept in my clothes."

Peter thought it best to ignore the comment.

The waitress set their drinks down on the table.

Peter glanced at his watch. *Where the hell is Stu?* He excused himself on the pretense of visiting the men's room. As soon as he was out of sight, he phoned Stu for his ETA and to give him a head's up on Louis' behavior.

Stu didn't sound the least bit concerned. "The guy's a virgin, business-wise. It sounds like he's experiencing first time jitters."

"Sure hope you're right."

"See you in a few."

* * *

Seated alone in the dimly lit lounge, Louis regretted his *faux pas,* revealing that he was under the care of a shrink. For most of his life, he'd struggled with mental illness, but the harder he tried to appear normal, the more elusive his goal became. By the time he'd reached puberty his family and friends had labeled him a "ding-dong." He'd flunked out of college and, supplemented by generous monetary gifts from his grandfather, drifted through a succession of boring, dead-end jobs.

His clinical diagnosis had run the gamut: attention-deficit, bipolar, generalized anxiety, and obsessive-compulsive disorders. Whenever he needed a break from the potpourri of prescribed mood stabilizers that produced unpleasant side effects, he self-medicated with booze and pot. His self-destructive behavior resulted in a never-ending roller coaster ride through elation and excess, alternating with debilitating depression.

Louis popped a Xanax into his mouth and washed it down with Scotch. *Letting Peter and Stu into my world of highs and lows is difficult enough, but without their guidance I'm just gonna screw up. Shit! I'm gonna blow it. Gotta keep it together.*

"Feeling more relaxed?" Peter asked, when he returned to the table and noticed Louis' shit-eating grin.

"Please forgive me. Whenever I travel I'm a bundle of nerves."

"Hey, buddy, no need to apologize. We all have our off days."

* * *

By the time Stu arrived, Louis had mellowed out. The rest of the evening was uneventful, except when Louis rigorously polished his knife and fork with his napkin, cut his steak into identical bite-sized morsels and lined the pieces up in rows.

Before dinner was over, the three men had struck a deal. They planned to meet with their lawyers the following week and draw up a contract.

The evening had left them exhausted. Instead of visiting the casino they decided to watch a Pay-Per-View sporting event in their suite.

No sooner had they entered the living area, Louis announced, "I'm beat. I'm turning in." He kicked off his shoes and left Peter and Stu staring at each other.

Stu whispered, "What were you so worried about? The guy's a pussycat."

"Yeah, sure, you weren't here when he freaked out. He's one crazy mixed-up pussycat."

"I'll take your word for it."

"If this deal goes through I'll need a place in Boca to hang my hat. Any suggestions?"

"You're welcome to stay in one of my luxury high-rise listings as long as you understand from time to time I show the property to clients."

"Fine with me as long as you give me enough time to put on my tighty-whities and shove the babes out of my bed."

"Not a problem. Think I'll turn in too. See you in the morning."

Peter entered his bedroom and stripped off his clothes. He adjusted the pillows on his bed and slid between the cool, crisp sheets. His body tingled with excitement. He imagined the endless possibilities that lay ahead.

Goodbye, Brooklyn.

Hello, Boca.

TEN

PETER AND STU RESURRECTED every piece of retired construction equipment they could lay their hands on.
The coughing and wheezing backhoes, bulldozers and grad-
ers were restored to vigorous health by a crew of mechanics
with dubious backgrounds having a difficult time finding
employment. The men didn't have a problem kicking back a
portion of their wages.

One of the mechanics introduced Peter and Stu to
Doug, a recovering alcoholic whose tainted reputation
made it impossible to find work as a structural engineer.
He expressed a willingness to turn a blind eye and a deaf
ear to minor infractions in exchange for the opportunity to
prove his worth as a general superintendent. He monitored
construction timeliness and compliance with state and local
building codes and fire regulations, as well as pitching in
whenever and wherever his services were needed.

Several projects had to be addressed before construction
began. A concrete wall was erected between the construction
site's far end and the Agricultural Preserve that abutted the
property. A thicket of sprawling ficus trees draped with
Spanish moss and towering slash pines offered a refuge for
nesting birds.

A double-sided billboard was installed on the main access road announcing the forthcoming Resort Lifestyle Community.

Landscaping had been deliberately left for last.

Peter and Stu huddled inside the construction trailer and considered proposals from landscape design specialists.

"I'm trying to avoid one of Louis' meltdowns," Peter said. "We don't want him to flip out after he hears South American Palms start at a whopping fifteen grand."

"Before that happens," Stu said, "I'll personally force-feed him his Xanax."

Their conversation was interrupted when Peter's phone rang.

"Hey J.J.," Peter said, "I was just about to call you."

"Never kid a kidder," J.J., their preferred landscape design specialist, replied.

"My hand to God, Stu and I were sitting around reviewing bids and we agreed, Jack Johnson's ahead by a nose."

"Great," J.J. said. "I have a feeling we speak the same language."

"What language is that?" Peter asked.

"I'm looking to expand my business and you're looking to save some dough and possibly skim a little off the top. Have I got that right?"

"You're my kinda guy, J.J."

"I guarantee you won't be disappointed."

The three men hammered out a sweet deal. J.J.'s plan included placing stately Queen Palms at the entrance and in front of the clubhouse where there's a need to impress, and clusters of less expensive Foxtails and Sabal Palmettos throughout the rest of the property. He'd bill for a greater number of imported trees, they'd divvy up the difference, and no one would be the wiser.

ELEVEN

EACH DAY BEFORE DAWN, PETER dispatched an unmarked van to the north county streets to pick up day laborers. There, Guatemalans, Hondurans, and Mexicans paced back and forth on separate corners, keeping a watchful eye out for police cruisers. With tool belts jangling, they ran alongside cars that slowed down, eager to negotiate a day's work for a fraction of what Americans earned.

"Give me a chance, *amigo*. Take me, I good worker." The men who weren't hired whined, "Shit, man, why you no pick me? Jus' wanna' sen' money to *mi familia.*"

Whenever the construction schedule fell behind, Doug, the project supervisor, would take the van out late Friday afternoon and pick an overnight crew. The men would work through the weekend. At night, they'd sleep on rough concrete floors with their heads resting on rolled-up jackets. Early Monday morning before the start of the new shift, Doug would drop them off back where he'd picked them up.

* * *

Whenever an inspector arrived at the construction site with the intention of beginning his workday in earnest, the day would begin with donuts and coffee accompanied by a lively debate about politics or sports with Director of Operations, Peter Duke. Afterwards, Doug would direct the inspector to the villas in the section under construction, where the entrances to the units were conveniently blocked with building materials and equipment. The inspector, inevitably, would opt for a comfortable alternative to navigating the obstacle courses: a leisurely, alcohol-fueled lunch at a restaurant of his choice.

They'd return by mid-afternoon with bleary eyes and bloated bellies. The inspector would stay just long enough to sign-off on the day's worksheets.

* * *

Peter targeted baby boomers with strategically placed real estate ads throughout the United States and Canada.

Stu recruited a team of top-notch real estate agents for the Hospitality Center. Each agent came with an impressive track record for closing the deal. The "sales consultants," as they came to be called, were required to wear casual dress that reflected Villa Paraiso's informal atmosphere.

Sales packets contained inviting images and enticing text, and promised a relaxed, dream-come-true lifestyle, a respite from winter's chill.

ESCAPE TO VILLA PARAISO

A PREMIER RESORT LIFESTYLE COMMUNITY
Your residential paradise located in desirable Boca Raton, Florida is convenient to cultural attractions, restaurants, shopping malls, houses of worship, major airports and major highways.

VILLA PARAISO offers a wide selection of Mediterranean-style villas with private courtyards.

The timeless beauty of Mediterranean-inspired architecture is expressed in the imaginative design of your spacious villa. Each villa reflects the informal South Florida lifestyle while maintaining Old World charm and casual elegance.

The creative application of mosaic medallions, natural stone and wrought iron, replicate the simplicity of 19th century architect Antonio Gaudi's respect for architectural detail and nature.

VILLA PARAISO offers the opportunity to fulfill your dreams in a relaxed atmosphere designed for the young and the young at heart. Enjoy lush tropical gardens, towering palm trees and amenities sure to satisfy your most diverse interests and pursuits, year-round.

DON'T MISS OUT ON THIS UNIQUE OPPORTUNITY!

TWELVE

NYPD DETECTIVE ED MARRONE first laid eyes on Vicky when he'd collared her for prostitution during Mayor Rudy Giuliani's massive Times Square cleanup. The other prosties begged and wailed, cursed and spit as the arresting officers herded them into police transfer vans. Vicky whimpered like a child, snot mixed with mascara smeared across the freckles on her button nose. Tawny-red hair framed her pale, thin face, her ample breasts too large for her waif-like frame. She reminded Ed of the naïve young women who arrived at Port Authority Bus Terminal from the heartland of America in search of excitement and often found more than they bargained for.

"Officer, please don't lock me up. I'm not like the rest of them," Vicky pleaded.

"*Well, looky looky,*" one of the other prostitutes said. "We've got ourselves a genuine Miss Goody Two-Shoes over here."

Laughter erupted from inside the van.

Before Ed slammed the doors shut, Vicky's pleading eyes had bored a hole in his soul. She'd ignited a spark that had died after he'd buried his wife the previous year. Love or lust, it didn't make a difference. His heart melted. He was hooked.

Ed learned that she had been on her own since she was a teenager. Her mother had stood by helplessly as Vicky's stepfather threw her out of their apartment with little more than the clothes on her back, a pocketful of change and nowhere to go.

After their initial encounter, Ed was consumed with the need to care for this person who had stolen his heart. He convinced Vicky to give up life on the street and move into his modest home on Staten Island.

Ed made an honest woman out of Vicky during a brief wedding ceremony at City Hall. Together, they made quite a sight. He, shorter and noticeably older than the bride-to-be; she, in a revealing white mini-dress and hooker heels from her working girl days.

It wasn't long before Vicky grew bored with playing house. She wasn't interested in cleaning and couldn't prepare a meal if her life depended on it. She watched mind-numbing soap operas or devoured celebrity gossip magazines whenever she wasn't shopping for clothes or cosmetics. Her shoe wardrobe rivaled that of Carrie Bradshaw.

Vicky had unlimited access to Ed's credit cards. Each time he confronted her about her shopping habits she fell to her knees and undid his fly. End of discussion.

He had to find a way to reduce his mounting credit card debt. Out of desperation, he took a part-time job as a private security guard. His first assignment was to escort a country western singer to an event at Radio City Music Hall.

Country gal admitted Ed to her hotel suite and dismissed her personal assistant. She gestured for him to sit down and disappeared behind richly carved, mahogany pocket-doors.

"Sheee-it!" she twanged from the next room.

Ed jumped up and ran to the door. "Is there a problem?"

The doors slid open. Country gal stood with one hand pulling at her ear lobe and the other hand pointing frantically. "Ah cain't fand mah airring. Ah think it rolled under the damn bed, but ah cain't fand it."

Ed crawled around on all fours until he spotted the enormous diamond stud, reached under the bed as far as possible, and scooped it up in his hand.

"You're a dear," she said before grabbing the earring and rewarding him with a big wet one.

The phone rang and she excused herself to answer the call in the next room.

Ed heard snippets of conversation that sounded like an admirer attempting to hook up with her later that night. He turned his attention to the gaping, velvet-lined jewelry case on top of the dresser. He'd only seen that much bling in the evidence room after a million dollar jewelry heist.

He mopped his brow with his handkerchief. *She can't possibly keep track of all this shit. She'll never miss one piece.* He grabbed a diamond-encrusted bracelet and slid it into his jacket pocket.

Country gal returned to the bedroom, her face flushed, no doubt as a result of the stimulating phone call. "All right sugar, we can go now."

Ed led the way. His sweaty palm slid off the doorknob. He turned to see if Country gal had noticed him perspiring profusely, but she was too busy air kissing her reflection in the mirror.

Ed fenced the swag with a retired police buddy whose life he'd saved back when they were rookies. He would have liked to have presented Vicky with the expensive piece of jewelry, but he needed the cash more than the mind-blowing "thank you" she'd surely bestow upon him.

* * *

During a mid-winter vacation, soaking up the sun along Miami's South Beach, Vicky surprised Ed with a tempting proposition. She promised to curtail her spending if he agreed to escape the big city's filth and crime and follow the sun. With thirty-three years on the job, Ed doubted he could change gears that easily until Vicky delivered her sales pitch straddling him, her 34DDs, a Christmas gift from an admirer in her previous life, bobbing like buoys guiding him to the Promised Land.

THIRTEEN

ED'S OLD HABITS HADN'T CHANGED much since he'd handed in his retirement papers and made the big move. He still slept with a police scanner squawking under his pillow and remained hyper-vigilant throughout the night.

"You're driving me nuts," Vicky said. "I expected you to stop listening to that damn thing after we left the city, but it's like you're addicted to it."

Ed pretended not to hear her.

She pounded her pillow. "I can't stand it anymore. If you don't get rid of that piece of crap, I'm sleeping in the guest room."

Ed mumbled an apology and turned off the sound. Moments later he closed his eyes and listened to Vicky's slow steady breathing, but sleep eluded him.

Startled by a noise coming from the rear of the house, he reached into his nightstand drawer and grabbed a flashlight and his backup revolver, a remnant from his NYPD days.

Vicky stirred.

"Shh," he said. "Stay here."

Ed cautiously made his way toward the screened patio. He pulled open the sliding glass doors and crouched as low as his protruding belly would allow.

He lunged forward. "Who the hell is out there? Answer me or I'll blow your balls off!"

He sensed someone behind him and turned to see Vicky stifling a giggle and pointing to his dangling manhood.

"Goddammit! You're lucky I didn't shoot you."

"What the hell are you doing?"

"Keep your voice down. I heard a noise back here."

She gave him the Italian salute punctuated with an erect middle finger and retreated to their bedroom.

Ed wasn't ready to return to bed before first securing the perimeter. He unlatched the patio's screen door and flung it open. His flashlight's beam cast an eerie glow. He shuddered as he stepped outside onto the damp grass. *I gotta look like a schmuck standing out here buck naked, waiving a gun.*

This was the defining moment when he realized he'd transitioned from decorated law enforcement officer to retired nobody, no title, no purpose, a non-entity.

The adrenaline rush continued to surge through his veins after he returned to bed. Too wound up to sleep, Ed stared at the ceiling and replayed the early days of their marriage when he'd nudge Vicky until she woke up and they'd make love. But now, they barely said "Good night." It wasn't her fault their love life had deteriorated. He was often too tired for sex, but it didn't seem to bother Vicky. Recently, she'd developed a new passion: jogging before dawn.

* * *

Vicky badgered Ed to pursue a hobby, or volunteer at a school or hospital, but working for free didn't appeal to him.

The one thing that did appeal to him was shooting the breeze with Murph, Villa Paraiso's Chief of Security.

On several occasions, Murph had invited Ed to accompany him on rounds. During a ride-along, Murph had been in the middle of telling Ed how one of his guys on night patrol had caught a couple screwing down by the pool. The story was interrupted when out of nowhere a customized pickup truck zoomed past from the opposite direction.

Murph made a quick U-turn and caught up with the truck before the internal road veered off toward the maintenance building. He put down his window and motioned for the driver to do the same.

The driver looked down from his elevated cab. "What's the problem?"

"Shit, Farley, how many times do I have to tell you?" Murph said. "You're not at a friggin' Monster Jam."

"What's the big deal? No one's on the goddamned road."

"Doesn't matter, it's a retirement community and I don't want to tell you again. Slow down!"

Farley mumbled something unintelligible and pulled away, tires squealing.

Murph put up his window. "Asshole. Rides around in that custom rig and thinks he owns the place."

"Does he live here?"

"Hell no, Farley's the maintenance supervisor. Rumor has it, he's got a lot of haters and I'm at the top of the list."

Ed nodded. "I can see why."

* * *

Vicky finally stopped nagging Ed to volunteer. Instead, she placed a copy of The Agenda where he'd be sure to see it, on the toilet seat lid in their master bathroom. One announcement had aroused his curiosity: *Men's Club Meeting at 10 a.m., First Tuesday of the Month, El Matador Meeting Room, Refreshments.*

He imagined a testosterone-charged event with conversations about sports and cars and without wives around to remind the men to take out the recyclables or change a light bulb. He promised himself he'd give it a try.

FOURTEEN

PEST STRIPS SPECKLED WITH INSECTS in various stages of decomposition dangled from the maintenance shed's bulletin board. A bright yellow announcement, posted in-between notices for used cars for sale and sleeping rooms for rent, caught Hector's attention:

WARNING!

A PROWLER HAS BEEN ROAMING THROUGHOUT THE COMMUNITY IN THE EARLY MORNING HOURS. REPORT ANY SUSPICIOUS ACTIVITY TO YOUR SUPERVISOR.

THE MANAGEMENT

A hand clamped down on Hector's shoulder. "Manny," he said, "wha' you doin'? You wanna scare me to death?"

"What's with you, scared of the bogeyman?"

"I wasn' spectin' nobody creepin' up on me."

"Hey take it outside!" Farley hollered.

Manny took a step backward and raised his hands. "You got it all wrong boss, we jus' talkin' about the notice."

Farley tapped the bulletin board with his red pen. "Management's been all over me about this problem. Duke wants maintenance to keep an eye out."

"Maybe is animal from behin' here, from Preserve," Hector said.

"I don't give a damn what it is," Farley said. "If I see it I'm gonna blow it to Kingdom Come! If I had my way, we'd all be packing a pistol." Farley pointed his index finger and thumb at the two men. "Pow! Pow!"

Manny elbowed Hector. "Then there's nothin' to worry about boss. You got it covered. See you *mañana.*"

Farley waived his pen in the air.

Manny tugged Hector's sleeve. "Hey man, wanna stop for a cold one on the way home?"

"No now."

The notice had rattled Hector to his core. He desperately needed to be alone. His sleeping room had often served as his sanctuary, but not today. Today, he felt like a caged animal. Instead of heading home, he slipped behind a recycling bin and waited until dark.

* * *

Hector's eyes tracked a pair of Ospreys silhouetted in moonlight as they flew overhead. A shrill, ear-splitting mating call pierced the still night moments before the graceful birds came to rest on a nearby nest.

To be free is not enough, Hector thought. *Birds mate… make family. I have no one to fill the emptiness in my heart, in my soul.*

A few feet away, he heard someone curse. A naked man threw open a screen door and stepped outside waving a gun.

Hector pressed his back against the villa and slid to the ground, tucked in his chin, and pulled his knees up tight against his chest. His ragged breath caught in his throat.

A narrow beam of light swept across the lawn and a few seconds later the screen door slammed shut.

Hector emerged from the shadows and stumbled blindly until he reached the wall separating the property from the Preserve. He stopped to catch his breath and gazed up at the sky. *Padre, I no deserve you forgive me, but I no can stop. I beg you… please, help me end this madness.*

FIFTEEN

AS A TEENAGER, RICK GOULD had daydreamed about becoming a musician, but it was his misfortune to excel in all things scientific. After he was accepted to Emory University School of Dentistry, he hoped his chosen profession would allow him time to pursue his interest in music.

Rick graduated with honors and opened a prestigious private practice in midtown Manhattan. He became a pioneer in dental implantation, shunned insurance companies and operated his practice on a strictly cash basis. This afforded him more latitude with the income he reported on his tax returns. It wasn't long before he found himself immersed in a lucrative specialty practice and with a growing family, his love of music was replaced with a new love: money.

Often, after Rick had dismissed his last patient for the day, he'd indulge in long sessions of self-administered nitrous oxide where sexual pleasure knew no boundaries. From his darkened Park Avenue office he'd peer through high-powered binoculars and observe unsuspecting guests cavorting in hotel rooms across the street. He'd breath in "sweet air" through the nose-inhaler attached to nitrous-oxygen tubing and stimulate his genitals into the wee hours of the morning.

After his marriage disintegrated and he and his wife divorced, he focused on pursuits that up until then he'd only fantasized about. He considered purchasing a sailboat or possibly one of those little sports cars his wife had insisted was impractical. Regardless of whether it was a BMW M3 or Porsche 911 one thing was certain: it had to be candy apple red.

* * *

Rick sifted through awards and honorary certificates he had accumulated during his illustrious career and discarded most of them in a trash bag. The mementos had meant little to him at the time he received them and meant nothing to him now. The remnants of his professional life now fit into a single carton, along with Villa Paraiso's sales brochure and a well-worn copy of *Florida Sportsman*.

He caressed a pair of binoculars before slipping them back into their scarred leather case and tried to ignore the gnawing sensation in his gut. *How the hell am I going to survive without my nitrous hits?*

He acknowledged that he might be a voyeur, but at least he didn't troll websites searching for porn like an out-and-out pervert.

The theme song from a popular TV show played in his head before he attempted his own rendition:

Bad boy, bad boy,
Whatcha' gonna do?
Whatcha' gonna do when the mood strikes you?
Bad boy, bad boy,
Whatcha' gonna do?
Whatcha' gonna do if there's no happy gas for you?

Before Rick flicked his office light switch for the last time, he gave a wistful look at the source of his late night pleasure, the five-star hotel across the way.

SIXTEEN

SEVEN NIGHTS a week, Boca's popular meet market, Artie's on the Bay, attracted a huge singles crowd hoping to score.

Rick chose a stool at the huge oval bar next to two moderately attractive women in their mid-fifties. He strained to hear their conversation over the live band's ear-splitting rendition of "Uptown Funk."

The willowy blonde whispered to the heavily made-up brunette sitting closest to Rick, "I see some new faces tonight." She gestured toward Rick. "Did you get a load of that one? Bet he has a few bucks. Expensive watch, looks like my grandfather's Patek Philippe and I can smell the Paco Rabanne from here. I say go for it."

The brunette turned toward Rick and fluttered her false eyelashes. "Hi. I'm Sherri.

"Rick."

"I don't recall seeing you here before. Are you on vacation?"

"I live in the area, but this is my first time at Artie's."

Sherri leaned in closer. "If I were making a guess, I'd say that you live in one of those fancy country club communities. Am I right?"

Rick stared at the ice melting in his drink. "You never know."

Sherri gushed, "You have a beautiful tan. I bet you own a boat."

"You must be psychic. Actually, I own two boats."

Her eyes widened. "Really, two boats?"

"Yeah, one's a rowboat and the other one is in the tub with my rubber ducky."

"Who the hell do you think you are?" Sherri didn't wait for a reply. She grabbed her drink and hurried to the opposite end of the bar.

Rick changed his seat several times before he realized more than a few women were knee-deep in their own brand of bullshit.

As the night wore on, he finally sprung for an $11.50 glass of Eco Domani in his attempt to reel in Lisa, a stunning brunette in her early twenties with the most exquisite emerald green eyes he'd ever seen. She wore a low-cut tank top, denim mini-skirt, and platform sandals that accentuated her long, tanned legs.

"So you're a premed student, I'm impressed."

She threw her head back and giggled. "Me too, I worked my ass off to get into the program at the university."

"I'm sure you did. How come you're not home hitting the books instead of hanging out here?"

"You know the old saying, all work and no play…"

Rick focused on the young woman's shimmering lips and imagined what a romp in the hay with her would be like. His genitals throbbed. *I feel like a horny teenager looking to get laid.*

"Tell me a little about yourself," Lisa said.

"I'm a retired dentist. I recently sold my practice up north and I'm ready to live the good life." *Almost time to close the deal.*

Lisa glanced toward the entrance. "Ah hah, well, you certainly picked the right place."

Suddenly their bantering ceased. Lisa grabbed her purse, pecked him on the cheek and made her way across the dimly lit room. She greeted a tall man with an athletic build, at least twenty years younger than Rick.

A hangdog expression covered Rick's face. *I would've been better off if I'd called an escort service or hit a single's mixer at the clubhouse.* He downed the rest of his drink and made a beeline for the parking lot.

* * *

Rick leaned back on the commode in his master bathroom and took a sip of Kona coffee. He reflected on his recent outing to the local meet market, capped off by his unsuccessful attempt to bed the luscious Lisa. *Have all these years sniffing nitrous screwed up my head? I'm a talented professional, but socially? Could be I'm too old for the young ones and it's time to move on to their mothers, or—God forbid— their grandmothers. Lord knows there are plenty of them out there hoping for one last hurrah.*

Rick took another sip of the robust brew and stared into the illuminated mirror that ran the length of the bathroom vanity. He saw an aging wannabe with puffy bags under his eyes and thinning, salt-and-pepper hair reflected back at him. *I need to cover this gray and start working out. And maybe it wouldn't be such a bad idea if I check out a mixer.*

He carried his empty mug to the den and skimmed through a stack of periodicals destined for the recycling bin. He located the current issue of *The Agenda* and thumbed through it until he found the *Singles' Events.* "Well what do we have here? Tonight at eight p.m., a singles' mixer in the Festival Lounge."

* * *

After Rick had showered and shaved and put on low-rise designer briefs, he devoted the better part of an hour to pulling shirts from his walk-in closet before tossing each one on the mountainous pile at his feet. Long sleeves, short sleeves, with a collar, without a collar, print, solid, none of them seemed right. The digital clock glared a warning. *Damn, it's almost 8:15 and I still can't make a decision. What's the big deal anyhow? It's not a job interview.*

If he hurried, he'd make it to the clubhouse by 8:30 p.m., a respectable time to arrive. Too early and he'd appear eager, later and he might miss the opportunity for a little action. He finally chose a blue, cotton print shirt, open at the collar, hanging loosely over a pair of perfectly creased dress denims. He stuffed his wallet into his pants pocket, grabbed his keys and iPhone and checked his watch. *Eight twenty-five… perfect.*

Rick took a deep breath and swaggered into the Festival Lounge. He excused himself before he eased his way between two small groups of smartly dressed women. He expected a warm welcome, but they were too busy jabbering to even notice him.

One of Dr. Phil's favorite expressions popped into his head. "How's that workin' for ya?"

Lose the attitude, buddy. From now on, you're nothing more than an average single guy trying to fill the long, lonely nights.

SEVENTEEN

GROWING UP, BETH COMPTON had enjoyed a childhood of excess, which included ballet lessons, expensive summer vacations, and private schools.

The summer before her senior year in college, she and Thomas, a handsome architectural student, met and fell in love. The events that followed were not unlike a fairytale. They became engaged, had a lavish wedding and received a spectacular gift from Beth's parents, a townhouse down the road from her childhood home. The couple welcomed their newborn son before their first anniversary.

Life appeared picture-perfect until one fateful day. Thomas had picked up their son from a birthday party and encountered a violent thunderstorm on the way home. The car skidded off the road and crashed through a guardrail.

Despite the coroner's assurance that both passengers were killed upon impact, Beth imagined they had suffered a horrible, painful death. She became despondent and eventually withdrew from the outside world.

Her parents had her admitted to a private psychiatric hospital where doctors prescribed an overzealous regimen of anti-depressants and electro-convulsive shock therapy.

* * *

Beth dangled her bare feet over the speckled linoleum floor that blended with the drab green walls the staff and patients often referred to as puke-green. She extended her leg and traced an invisible pattern with her toe.

The aide pulled an outfit from the closet and held it out to her. "Mmm hmm. Your parents sure sent over some pretty things. It's such a nice day outside. Why don't we wear something colorful? How 'bout this here purple one?"

Beth shook her head.

The aide returned the outfit to the closet and continued to rummage. "Robin's egg blue, now that's your color, matches your pretty blue eyes." She held up another hanger. "How 'bout this one?"

Again Beth shook her head.

"Girl, you know the rules. You have to get dressed."

Beth repeatedly twisted the sash on her bathrobe around her fingers. "Mother's Day…"

"What about Mother's Day, hun?"

"My husband… my son Bobby…"

"I know it ain't been easy for you, but you can't keep hidin' in your bathrobe. Don't matter none if it's a present from your loved ones." The aide undid the sash and guided Beth's limp arms through the sleeves. "Robin's egg blue it is."

* * *

Beth's parents had spent a considerable amount of money for Beth's private hospital stay. Noticing little improvement in her condition, they agreed that she needed the love and support of her family and community more than hospitalization. They believed that their church offered a pathway to healing and were certain that if Beth reconnected with her faith, her spirit would be renewed.

During Sunday Mass, Sister Angela focused her attention

on the listless parishioner staring off into space. Her curiosity increased at the social hour that followed. She watched as an older, solicitous couple made certain the woman was never without a brimming cup of coffee and an overflowing plate of sweets.

In the week that followed, Sister Angela found herself thinking about the young woman that had caught her attention. On a blustery Friday afternoon, Mother Superior suggested that a glass of sherry is just what they needed to relieve their mutual head colds. One glass led to another as they whiled away the afternoon chatting. Sister Angela inquired about the parishioner she had observed at the coffee social. Despite Mother Superior's slurred speech and muffled yawns, it didn't take long before the family's sad tale unfolded.

At the next coffee social, Sister Angela engaged the woman who had piqued her interest in conversation. "It's so nice to see you again."

The woman offered a wan smile. "Thank you."

"I don't recall seeing you before last week."

"I've... I've been away."

* * *

Over the next few months, Beth and Sister Angela's friendship blossomed. Eventually Sister Angela confided her own feelings of despair and loneliness.

She had survived an awkward childhood, the only girl in a family of four boys. She engaged in rough-house play, shunned ruffled pinafores and preferred to wear well-worn flannel shirts and blue jeans like her brothers. Her parents feared she'd surely succumb to the temptation of the devil and end up a lesbian unless drastic steps were taken.

Her mother had stood before her, hands on hips, her

coal, black eyes piercing Angela's soul. "What do you mean, you won't go?"

"You can't make me."

"Don't you know you're on a path headed straight to Hell?"

"I haven't done anything wrong," the child pleaded. "I help with the chores, get good grades in school. I never miss Sunday Mass."

"That's not enough. You must seek redemption for your troubled soul. Only by serving the Lord will you receive his grace and be forgiven for your sins."

"Ma, please."

"Hush, I won't hear another word."

Shortly after their confrontation, Angela's mother sent her off to an obscure Catholic order several hours away from home.

Sister Angela began her life of silent misery as an unwilling participant in abstinence, devotion, prayer, and donning the vestments her faith dictated, all the while pretending to be something she wasn't.

* * *

Beth and Sister Angela sat next to each other at the next coffee social. Beth's parents were seated across the room engaged in conversation with another couple.

"I have money, you know," Beth whispered. "In fact, quite a lot of money. I have the settlement from my husband's life insurance policy and after I repay my parents for my hospital stay, I'd like to do something for *me*."

Sister Angela wasn't sure how to respond. "That's nice dear. Perhaps you'll sail away in a pea-green boat and dance by the light of the moon."

Hearing a line from her son Bobby's favorite nursery

rhyme, *The Owl and the Pussy Cat,* brought tears to Beth's eyes. "You're mocking me."

Sister Angela patted Beth's hand. "Oh dear, I didn't mean to. But you never know. One day, perhaps we'll sail away together."

A short time later, a parishioner returned from visiting relatives in South Florida and was eager to share her experience along with the brochure expounding Villa Paraiso's idyllic lifestyle.

Sister Angela and Beth agreed that the prospect of living in a villa in a tropical paradise sounded like the perfect way to begin their new lives.

* * *

Angela tiptoed down the hall leading to the bedrooms and opened her housemate's door a crack. She watched the sleeping woman's thin summer blanket rise and fall with each breath. In the short time they had shared their living space Angela had become increasingly fond of this unfortunate soul. She opened the door all the way. "Hey sleepy head, time to get up."

Beth stretched her arms over her head and peered at the bedside clock. "Mmm… Angela is that you? It's only nine-thirty." She pulled the blanket over her head to block out the sunlight.

"I'm making French toast, just the way you like, with cinnamon and vanilla."

"I'm not hungry."

"Come on now, you remember what your doctor said? You can't stay in bed all day and you have to eat. You don't want to go back to that psych hospital, do you?"

Beth huddled a moment longer before she tossed back the blanket. "Okay, okay, but I'll need a few minutes."

Angela closed the door and returned to the kitchen.

Beth sat up and rubbed her eyes. She reached over and lifted a framed photo of her husband and son from the nightstand and pressed it to her breast. "My darlings," she whispered, tears streaming down her cheeks, "I pray each night for God to take me while I sleep. I'm nothing without you… nothing." She kissed the picture and placed it back on the nightstand.

EIGHTEEN

JAY FRIEDLANDER SLOUCHED in his desk chair and stared out at the dismal gray sky. He hated winter: the icy roads, shoveling snow, and digging out his car. It wasn't unusual to discover that during the night, a sanitation truck had plowed the road and buried the parked cars, his included. He wondered if his winter doldrums signaled the beginning of a midlife crisis.

The dry office air parched his throat. A stack of pink "while you were out" message slips begged for attention. He considered pushing everything off his desk onto the floor and leaving the mess for the janitor to dispose of, but what would that accomplish?

He pulled over a journal marked *Fund Raising* and studied the entries. Proceeds from the student-operated café and holiday bazaars consisted of cash transactions. Most of the items sold there were donated by local merchants. No one would be the wiser if he pilfered a portion of the funds. It would be easy enough to record lesser amounts in a duplicate journal. He didn't need the money, but thinking about stepping outside his comfort zone lifted his spirits.

A soft knock on the door brought him back to reality. He slammed the journal shut. "Come in, door's unlocked."

His secretary, Beverly, entered his office carrying a bulging briefcase and a small bunch of artificial flowers.

"I was on my way out and I noticed light coming from under your door. I'm not interrupting am I?"

Jay shook his head. "What's with the flowers?"

"I think I have an admirer. He's a third grader."

"Then I wouldn't worry about it developing into a long-term relationship. Hey, you're working kind of late yourself."

Beverly's shoulder-length curls bounced as she spoke. An impish grin appeared on her face. "Have to submit end of the month reports in a timely fashion. Wouldn't want my principal to put a letter in my file now, would I?"

"I'd never do that to you."

Prior to that afternoon, Jay had indulged in a mild flirtation with the attractive woman in her late-thirties. He'd been careful not to overstep personal and professional boundaries.

Jay found Beverly's smile disarming. He took her briefcase and flowers, placed them on a nearby chair and helped her out of her coat. He brushed her lips with his fingertips and pulled her close, flicked the light switch off and locked the door.

* * *

After Jay's life of adultery and petty crime had begun, it didn't take long before his persona changed. He felt energized and looked forward to each day with renewed interest. That was until the school auditors arrived.

Jay had endured a grueling week observing auditors scrutinize his records. Beverly had suggested he come to her place for a light supper. On the way home, she stopped by the local deli and picked up barbecued chicken, potato salad, and two crusty rolls.

Jay arrived shortly before 6 p.m., grateful for the opportunity to put the ongoing audit out of his mind and relax.

"This must've been a rough week for you," Beverly said, picking at her food.

"You have no idea."

"I... I've had kind of a rough week myself."

Jay put down his knife and fork. "Oh?"

"I know this isn't the best time, but—"

"What, what's wrong?"

"I'm pregnant."

"That's not possible. I've got auditors on my back and now this. How the hell did it happen?"

"How did it happen? Remember Sex Ed 101, the egg, the sperm."

"You told me you're on the pill or was that a lie?"

"Oh Jay, how can you accuse me of lying to you? I'm just as upset about this as you are."

He shook his head. "I don't get it. Enlighten me."

"A couple of times I... I guess I forgot to take it."

Jay came around the table and placed his hand over Beverly's belly. "With everything that's going on at work, I lost it. Sorry. We'll get through this... together."

* * *

After the auditors uncovered discrepancies in Jay's record keeping, further investigation was necessary before a disciplinary hearing could be scheduled. For the next six months he was reassigned to what his co-workers referred to as the "rubber room." During this time, his wife filed for divorce and announced that she and their children planned to move across the country to be near her parents.

Jay had not only ruined his former wife's and his children's lives, he had made a mess of Beverly's life and his career, as well. He had descended from a position of integrity and trust, risked losing his pension and faced the possibility of criminal prosecution.

* * *

Finally, the charges against Jay were dropped due to insufficient evidence. Jay assumed he was home-free, but his union rep's off-the-record comments sent him reeling.

"You're a lucky man."

"Yeah, yeah, when can I get back to work?"

"Hold on a minute. You're lucky your picture isn't on the front page of the newspaper, but that's where your luck runs out."

"What in hell are you talking about?"

"It has been strongly suggested that you consider early retirement... effective immediately."

"What?" Jay said. "What about a transfer? Surely that's a possibility. I'm willing to accept a position in another district."

"Sorry pal. This is the end of the line for you. You've been told to get lost."

* * *

Beverly pointed at her profile reflected in the mirror and shook her head. "You look like a balloon in the Thanksgiving Day parade," she said aloud.

Jay called from the next room. "Are *you* talking to me?"

Beverly appeared in the doorway. "No, *Daddy*, but..." She pointed to her bulging baby bump. "I'm about ready to pop, or haven't you noticed?"

"Of course, I've noticed, but for the past six months I've been busy trying to save my ass or haven't *you* noticed?

Beverly burst into tears.

Jay tried to put his arms around her, but she pushed him away.

He tried again. This time she offered no resistance. He tilted her chin upward and gazed into her eyes. "I'm sorry for everything, I love you." He put his hand on her belly. "I love both of you."

She stopped crying. "And…"

"And what?"

She held her hands out, palms up. "And what else?"

Jay burst out laughing. "Oh, you mean like, 'will you marry me?'"

"For a principal you're not very bright."

"Former principal, but I don't have to be bright."

"Oh, why's that."

"I have you to guide me."

NINETEEN

FOLLOWING THE BIRTH of their daughter, Jay had shed copious amounts of tears. When he first glimpsed the helpless bundle of humanity, she was hooked up to monitors, and a nasal gastric tube protruded from her tiny nose.

The incessant "beeping," the pulsating symphony linking life and death, convinced Jay that heaven offered the merciful solution for their SPMR infant, doctor-speak for severely and profoundly mentally retarded.

Beverly's parents had been visibly upset when they found Jay seated at her bedside. One look at their pinched lips told him what they were thinking. *You bastard, you ruined our daughter's life. God has punished you. You got what you deserve.*

Jay had begged doctors not to employ extraordinary means and to forgo heroic measures. "Let her go, let her die in peace," he pleaded, but the Hippocratic Oath, ethical and legal issues took precedence. The solution: a sedative administered to the overwrought father.

Reality was a bitter pill for Beverly to swallow. She found it impossible to accept that her uterus had expelled this tiny flawed human being.

She declined an orderly's offer to wheel her to the

Neonatal Intensive Care Unit. "I can't bear to see her hooked up to machines. What's the point?"

The orderly placed a comforting hand on her arm. "In a situation like this there's no right or wrong answer, but it's possible, later on, you'll regret your decision."

Reluctantly, Beverly agreed to visit her daughter in the NICU, but only if she viewed the infant from afar.

* * *

Jay and Beverly spent the next several months visiting their fragile infant in the hospital before they were permitted to take their daughter home. It didn't take long before they realized how ill-equipped they were to cope with a special needs child. After much soul-searching, they placed their daughter in a residential care facility in upstate New York.

Jay kept busy tutoring college students and Beverly registered with a temp agency.

The emotional and physical chasm between them grew wider with each passing day. They avoided each other whenever possible. On one rare occasion, they sat on opposite sides of the sofa and watched a TV show together in which a town was overrun with zombies.

"I feel like a zombie," Jay said during a commercial break.

"What do mean?"

"I'm dead inside."

"You think you're the only one?"

"No, I suppose not, but I'm worried that if we continue like this, whatever is left of our marriage will disintegrate."

Endless discussion and debates ensued until they agreed to a fresh start in new surroundings. Leaving a piece of their hearts behind wouldn't be easy, but they were willing to give it a try.

TWENTY

SANDY MELCHER hadn't realized how exhausted she was until the moving van pulled away. She let out a heavy sigh and closed the door behind her.

She sat down cross-legged on the tile floor between the dining area and kitchen and watched her sister, Eleanor, climb up and down the step-ladder. Deciding where to place their grandmother's delicate china and crystal was not a job Sandy wanted any part of. However, she did feel a twinge of guilt until she reminded herself that she was the one who had researched retirement communities, and attended to all the details, before they moved to Villa Paraiso.

Convincing Eleanor to relocate had not been easy. "Why don't you want to talk about it? Scared you'll start bawling?"

Eleanor sniffled, "Maybe."

"You're such a crybaby. Grow up."

"I don't like change and I'm perfectly content to stay right where I am. Everything I need is practically outside our front door... museums, theatres and the best hospitals in the country."

"Do you hear yourself? Hospitals? What about ceme-teries? We have some lovely cemeteries. And how often do you visit a museum or attend a Broadway show? You sound ridiculous."

The day "Sully" Sullenberger had successfully ditched his passenger plane on the Hudson River, Eleanor became overwhelmed with what-ifs. What if he had misjudged and a wing clipped their apartment building? What if he had hit their building head-on? She resorted to taking three milligrams of Lunesta at bedtime to silence her obsessive thoughts.

Sandy interpreted the incident as an omen. Perhaps it was time to retire and move out of the city. She certainly wouldn't miss the constant subway delays or perverts flashing their goods.

Neither of them had married. Throughout their lives, they had relied on each other. With their combined social security checks, Sandy's pension from AT&T and a tidy little nest egg, they were optimistic about the future.

Eleanor reluctantly agreed to move on one condition: that Sandy do the research and make all the arrangements.

* * *

Sandy tore open a carton that contained the remnants of their family's history. She thumbed through a leather-bound photo album, a reminder of the story their mother often recited before her beauty and memory faded into oblivion:

November 1911, the S.S. Rijndam sailed from Rotterdam, Holland to America.

A young man noticed a woman puking over the railing. Onlookers avoided the woman in distress until the man pulled a dingy rag from his pocket and offered it to her.

The young woman took the cloth, but instead of wiping her mouth, she held it at arm's length. "This shmatta is filthy. You offer such shmutz to a lady?"

"My handkerchief is not good enough to clean vomit?" He grabbed the rag from the woman's hand and pretended to blow his nose. "Now that's disgusting."

They both laughed as he held the handkerchief between his thumb and forefinger and tossed it over the side of the ship.

The woman wiped her hand on her skirt before she extended it. "I'm Dora. Thank you for coming to my aid."

The man bowed slightly. "You are most welcome. It is my pleasure."

They gazed into each other's eyes, immersed in their own private thoughts, until the man broke the silence.

"I almost forgot. My name is David."

"You forgot your name is David?"

"No, it's just that—" David blushed before he realized she was teasing.

During the long, harsh voyage, David and Dora discovered that they had both lived on the outskirts of Czernonrtz in Austria, he to the north, she to the south. They exchanged stories of loved ones left behind and shared their hopes and dreams for the future. They stole a kiss or a tender caress whenever they were certain no one was looking. By the time the Statue of Liberty came into view, David and Dora had declared their love for each other. Three months later they married and not long after, Eleanor's grandmother was born.

"Oh, my God! Sandy, come here, quick!"

Sandy looked up expecting to find her sister sprawled on the floor. Instead, Eleanor stood perfectly still with her shaking finger pointed at the sink, her ashen face frozen with fear.

Sandy jumped up and ran to her sister's side. "This is what you're afraid of, this innocent little thing that's not bothering anyone? She reached over to grab the baby lizard by its tail and caught a glimpse of someone peeking out at her a moment before their shutters snapped shut.

"You'd better get used to this," she said and dangled the lizard in her sister's face.

Eleanor recoiled. "Eek! Get that monster away from me."

"Welcome to Florida," Sandy said, as she opened the front door and tossed the monster onto the grass.

TWENTY-ONE

AL FRANK RETURNED HOME to find two moving men unloading the contents of a long-distance van onto the sidewalk across the street. A woman he surmised was the new owner appeared to be supervising them. He dropped his shopping bags on the floor in his entry foyer and peered out from between slats of stark white Bermuda shutters. He had acquired the habit of seeing without being seen as a resident of The City That Never Sleeps.

Nice lookin' broad, Al thought. I'll let her settle in before I inquire if there's a husband tucked away somewhere. He scooped up the bags and hurried to his bedroom, anxious to try on his new acquisitions.

The saleslady had assured him that colorful walking shorts and coordinated shirts were the latest style, sure to please the ladies.

One advantage of living in a tropical climate was dressing like an exotic bird without attracting negative attention. His co-workers back home would have split their sides laughing if they'd seen him in his snazzy new wardrobe.

Al slipped into a pair of docksiders, *sans* socks, and tugged at his turquoise and yellow Tommy Bahama shirt, size XXL. He hoped that the side-slits and bold tropical pattern would do much to camouflage his bulging midsection. He needed all the help he could get if he hoped to change his status, from life-long loser in the romance department to the guy who scores.

He returned to the front window, hoping to continue his observation unobserved. The truck had already pulled away and his new neighbor was nowhere in sight. Al was startled by a face pressed against the window across the way. He snapped his shutters closed and hoped his snooping had gone undetected.

* * *

Al had started working at his mind-numbing bus driver's job with the Manhattan Transit Authority straight out of high school. During his off hours, he tended to his ailing mother. Over time, his love for her was replaced by resentment. There were times he felt overwhelmed and wailed, "Betty, why don't you die already?" But afterwards, he was filled with remorse.

Many a Saturday night he had dozed in front of the TV, a half-eaten bag of cheese puffs spilling onto the floor. He'd awaken in the middle of the night and drag himself off to bed.

One Wednesday each month, he'd squeeze his corpulent body into an ill-fitting, outdated suit he had purchased for his father's funeral ten years earlier. He'd wait until he was certain his mother was asleep before sneaking out of the house. Then, he'd walk the dozen or so blocks to the singles' dance held in Our Lady of Fortunata's gymnasium, where for ten dollars he'd feast on freshly baked cookies and fruit punch, and pray that *his* God wouldn't punish him for attending a *church* social.

Al dreaded the rejection he had experienced at previous

dances. In one particularly painful incident he overheard two women whispering to each other.

"He's coming this way," one woman had said, shielding her mouth with her hand, but loud enough for him to hear. "I hope he doesn't ask *me* to dance."

The other woman had frowned. "He looks like a *loser.*"

The two women hurried across the dance floor and left him standing alone.

I'm a man, put on earth to satisfy a woman and propagate the species. Propagate? I'd be happy if a woman agreed to dance with me. If only they'd give me a chance.

* * *

After Al's mother died from complications due to pneumonia, her attorney informed him that between annuities, insurance policies and the three-story Brownstone he'd lived in his entire life, he was now financially independent.

Without responsibilities, and with his inheritance assured, he was free to leave his humdrum life behind.

Al had read a magazine article extolling the virtues of South Florida living where women outnumbered men five-to-one. He represented a commodity in high demand, a single man who loved to dance and drove at night.

He was anxious to replace his outdated wardrobe with sportswear designed to hide out-of-shape middle-aged men's imperfections and embark on the adventure of a lifetime.

After a brief period of mourning, Al sold his house and its contents and purchased the car of his dreams, a brand new Caddy convertible. He loaded up his personal belongings and headed to the Sunshine State.

* * *

Al awoke to see glorious sunshine streaming through his hotel window. He stood out on the balcony and breathed in salty air. His stomach rumbled. He skipped the shower and dressed hastily. On the way to the café adjacent to the pool, he grabbed a complimentary newspaper in the hotel lobby. He downed two glasses of freshly squeezed orange juice and scoured the real estate section.

Villa Paraiso's full-page ad caught his attention. He scoffed down a deluxe breakfast, retrieved his car from the valet, and made it to Boca Raton in record time.

TWENTY-TWO

AS SOON AS AL WAS SETTLED IN, he made a bee-line for the clubhouse. He approached the member services' desk with the intention of inquiring about singles' events. Two women maneuvered their way in front of him. *Who do these gals think they are?* "Excuse me ladies, perhaps you didn't notice. I'm ahead of you."

"Ooh!" the seductive redhead cooed and flipped her hair back. "I'm so, so sorry."

Al stroked his fleshy jowls. *These gals are past their prime, but their plastic surgeon is a miracle worker.* He inhaled the redhead's intoxicating fragrance. Despite her advanced age, he felt himself becoming aroused. "I'm Al… Al Frank, recently arrived from The Big Apple, and you are…?"

The women giggled like schoolgirls at their first co-ed dance. "You won't believe this," the redhead gushed, "but I'm Mary and she's Jane." Mary pointed a purple fingernail decorated with tiny rhinestones at herself and then at her friend. "You know, like the candy."

Al endured another round of giggles accompanied by the women elbowing each other.

Mary reached over to a Lucite display and removed three copies of The Agenda. She handed one to Al. "Since you're new here, you'll need one of these. It's the Bible we live by. She clutched the bulletin to her enhanced bosom. "If not for this, we'd wither away and die."

Al arched an eyebrow. He doubted that these two gals relied on a monthly bulletin for personal fulfillment. "You're kidding, right?"

The duo winked at each other and then at Al.

He watched as they teetered down the hall, their mile-high heels click-clacking along the way, their flabby asses stuffed into spandex leggings, undulating like sailboats on a breezy day. He remained transfixed until the women turned, struck an alluring pose and blew air kisses in his direction.

He let out a long wolf whistle and headed toward the clubhouse lobby.

The contemporary furnishings, ordered from a Scandinavian catalog, offered little in the way of comfort. The chairs were too narrow, the sofas too low. Nothing was designed to accommodate his bulky physique until he came across an upholstered bench outside the men's bathroom.

After Al thumbed through *The Agenda,* he understood the importance of this invaluable resource. Classes, clubs, cultural programs, live entertainment, socials… His mind reeled. Deciding which events to participate in would be difficult, but he was certain of one thing. Based on his encounter with Mary and Jane he was beginning to think of himself in a whole new way.

TWENTY-THREE

EACH SUNDAY MORNING, after her daughter and son-in-law had deserted her, Rebecca Ehrlich waited for the phone to ring. When it did, the ensuing conversations often ended with Miriam, her daughter, accusing her of being stubborn. Maybe she was right, but Rebecca was determined to live out what was left of her life in familiar surroundings.

The few friends that had lived in her building had either moved closer to their adult children or were resting peacefully in a cemetery. Most of the apartments were now home to crack-heads and other undesirables. Rebecca was one of the few remaining original tenants in a decaying, vermin-infested Bronx tenement.

She'd wasted countless hours on the phone complaining to management about the lack of heat and hot water. She had given up complaining about falling plaster and ineffective pest control, and the malfunctioning elevator that creaked and shuddered during her infrequent ventures into the outside world.

After Rebecca had threatened to call the Housing Authority and report her deplorable living conditions, to include that rodents threatened to overrun her tiny apartment, a man who identified himself as Property

Manager Peter Duke paid her a surprise visit. He hastily walked from room to room and made a few notes on a scrap of paper. Before he departed, he promised to follow-up on her complaints, but warned her to stop making trouble or he would have her evicted.

Rebecca listened for the cacophony of clanking radiators, but they remained silent. She tugged at the shawl collar on her frayed chenille robe and dabbed at her nose with a tissue.

She shuffled down the narrow hallway toward the kitchen, grabbed a soup ladle, and banged on an ice-cold radiator. Gnarled knuckles and angry blue veins strained under transparent skin. Her frustration dissolved into tears.

It wouldn't be long before her arthritic spine surrendered to the absence of steam heat and she'd be immobilized for the rest of the day. She retreated to a straight-back chair and waited, her hands tightly folded in her lap.

Rebecca was no stranger to pain. She had only to glance at the faded numbers tattooed on her left forearm to trigger unspeakable horrors. Words were unnecessary. *4-2-3-5-7-9* spoke volumes.

Her hollow eyes defied the terrifying dreams and paralyzing fear that haunted her nights. She had witnessed atrocities through the eyes of a seven-year-old child, her family torn from their beds in the middle of the night, dragged into the street, pleading... screaming... the deafening crack of gunfire... and finally... silence.

* * *

Miriam and her husband Aaron sat propped up in their king-sized Craftmatic adjustable bed with individual remote controls. The Sunday paper lay strewn across the imported, hand-stitched linen duvet that matched the obscene collection of decorative pillows tossed haphazardly onto the plush carpeting.

Miriam dreaded making the weekly phone call to her mother. Despite her mother's having been emotionally unavailable when Miriam was growing up, Miriam was sincere in her desire for her mother to experience a better quality of life.

As a child, Miriam would run home from school anxious to relate the day's events and often found her mother staring into space unable or unwilling to open her heart to a child who desperately yearned for affection.

Rebecca hesitated before lifting the receiver on her end. She disliked the predictable Sunday morning tug-of-war, but if she failed to answer the phone, Miriam would alert 9-1-1.

"Hello, Mommy," Miriam said in a small voice.

She's still my little girl, Rebecca thought, savoring the moment she knew would be short-lived.

"Mother, why did you take so long to answer the phone?"

"You think it's easy for your old mother to shuffle over to the telephone?"

"You make yourself sound so… so… frail, so helpless. You're not, you know. Why do you act as if you're so fragile? Do you do it to gain sympathy?"

Rebecca never understood her daughter's frustration. Miriam's disparaging remarks sounded like selfish whims. *What does she want from me? I cooked, I cleaned. I was home waiting for her every day after school.*

"Nu, here we go again."

"What do you mean, here we go again?" Miriam said. "Do you think I like living so far away, worrying if you're warm enough, if you're well, or if someone mugged you and you're lying in a hospital bed unconscious?"

"My darling daughter, you've always had a flair for melo-drama."

"If you lived down here with us you wouldn't suffer as

much with your arthritis and you'd enjoy your life more. In fact you'd have a life. What you have now is barely an existence."

Rebecca shook her head. "*Oy, oy, oy!*"

"I'll speak to you next week, mother. Hopefully, you'll reconsider your decision. Until then, stay well."

"Yes, *Mammaleh*, I'll think about your offer and then I'll think some more, and my answer will still be the same. No, I'm not moving."

"Goodbye, Mother."

"Goodbye, Miriam."

Miriam turned to Aaron. "That's it. I've had it. There's only one way to get Mother down here."

Aaron had been working on the *New York Times* crossword puzzle, but it became impossible to concentrate with the drama unfolding next to him. He frowned. "We're going to kidnap her?"

"Very funny, but no. We're going to have her evicted."

Aaron snapped his head back. "You're not serious?"

"I'm damn serious."

"And just how do you expect that to happen?"

"Don't mail in her rent check. In fact, inform her landlord that you refuse to pay for substandard living conditions and while you're at it, tear up Mother's monthly allowance check." Miriam gleefully rubbed her hands together.

"That's cruel, Miriam. We're talking about your mother, not some stranger."

"Well, she leaves me no choice."

TWENTY-FOUR

BEFORE LUXURIATING IN A STEAMY, pulsating shower, Bunny Levin dimmed the bedroom light and tossed her strawberry-blonde wig carelessly onto the bed. On her way to the bathroom, she avoided looking at her naked reflection in the mirrored dressing room. The scent of honey and vanilla filled the air. The foaming body wash she had purchased at Neiman-Marcus had been well worth the exorbitant price tag.

Seated in front of the vanity mirror adorned with gilded cherubs, Bunny snuggled into a thick, pink bath towel and scrutinized her image. Her overwhelming sense of isolation brought back memories of her classmates incessant teasing about her oversized front teeth. The nickname Bunny had followed her into adulthood.

She brushed her hand across sparse tufts of chestnut-brown hair poking out of her scalp and continued across the bridge of her nose and alongside her cheek. Her index finger glided back and forth across pouting lips, making wider and wider circles that ended at her delicate neck. She allowed the towel to slip down around her waist and expose her boyish chest. Angry red scars mocked her. She recoiled in disgust.

Bunny had had her share of sexual encounters with men, but it had been a long time since she'd been intimate. *How will I respond to a man's touch? What if he's repulsed by what he sees?* She shielded her scars with her hands and burst into tears.

* * *

Naïve and inexperienced, Bunny had fumbled through her sexual awakening with a distant cousin visiting her aunt for the summer. A few months before her seventeenth birthday, she discovered she was pregnant.

Her ultra-Orthodox Jewish parents banished her from their home. She had stood on their stoop, a large paper sack tossed haphazardly at her feet. Her father ranted loud enough for the neighbors to hear, "*Kurvah!* Whore!" before he slammed the door shut.

Her family sat *shiva,* the ritual reserved for mourning the dead, but an elderly aunt took pity on Bunny and invited her to live in the basement in exchange for help with cooking and cleaning.

After Bunny's pregnancy ended in a miscarriage, her aunt encouraged her to attend secretarial school, which she offered to pay for.

Bunny was tenacious in her attempt to reinvent herself. She emulated the elegant women featured in fashion magazines. By the time she graduated, she'd evolved into a confident, sophisticated young woman. Eventually, she married a partner at the law firm where she worked.

* * *

Bunny had endured thirty years in a miserable, childless marriage when she was diagnosed with Stage III, bilateral breast cancer. Following a debilitating course of chemotherapy and radiation, she discarded her husband along with her breasts.

She had a difficult time accepting her mutilated body, but reconstructive surgery wasn't an option. Friends attempted to console her, but the pity she heard in their words and saw in their eyes made her feel that much more inadequate.

One gloomy winter morning, Bunny gave into a bout of self-pitying and remained in bed for most of the day. From time to time, she glanced at the newspaper. A full-page real estate ad caught her attention. It captured the essence of a tropical paradise located on Florida's Gold Coast. The resort lifestyle community offered an escape to a destination where no one knew her or her history.

The following morning, Bunny reserved a flight to West Palm Beach and booked an oceanfront hotel room. In between dips in the surf and sightseeing, she visited Villa Paraiso's sales center and toured the property. Before she had completed the tour, she was ready to sign on the dotted line.

TWENTY-FIVE

THE WOMEN'S CLUB MEETING wasn't scheduled to begin for another half-hour, but more than half the chairs were occupied. The room was abuzz with the latest gossip and restaurant reviews.

Beverly preferred to sit with Angela and Beth despite the nasty rumors about their relationship. She was grateful they didn't invade *her* privacy by asking questions that made her feel uncomfortable; questions about how a mother abandons her fragile child.

Angela gestured for Beverly to sit in the empty chair next to her.

"Aren't you saving the seat for Beth?" Beverly asked.

"No," Angela said. "She won't be joining us today."

"That's too bad. She's such a sweetheart. She's not sick is she?"

She's lost interest in socializing. "Nothing serious," Angela said, "she's just a little under the weather."

"Now that I think about it, I haven't seen either of you at dinner recently."

She's lost her appetite. "We've been eating at home more."

"Please tell Beth I asked for her and I hope she feels better soon."

Angela forced a smile. *If only it were that easy. I'm worried her depression is returning and I don't have a clue how to head it off.*

Bunny, Vicky, and several new members sat at a nearby table. One of the chubby new members leaned in and addressed the other women at the table, "Have any of you eaten at Paul's Grille?"

"Paul's Grille… crab cakes to die for," her equally plump tablemate chimed in.

"Mamma Mangia," Vicky said. "Now that's the place you wanna try. Humongous portions. You share one dinner and have enough left over for a *dawgie* bag."

Several women at the table looked at Vicky disparagingly.

Bunny rolled her eyes at the garishly attired "Noo Yawker," the nickname many of the residents called Vicky behind her back.

A painfully thin woman dressed in exercise garb glanced sideways. "Enough about food already, did you see who just walked in?"

Everybody at the table turned toward the entrance and gawked.

One of the new members strained to see who they were staring at. "I didn't bring my glasses, who're you talking about?"

The thin woman hissed, "Those sluts, you know the ones. Look at the two of them prancing in here like circus ponies. I wouldn't be caught dead in one of those outlandish get-ups."

Mary and Jane were giggling when they entered the room, oblivious to the stares and whispers from several of the women.

Jane sneered. "Looks like we've arrived at the Isle of Lesbos."

Mary noticed that most of the empty chairs were occupied by purses. "And the cliques have staked their claims."

The two women helped themselves to coffee. Jane brushed poppy seeds off a pre-sliced bagel and proceeded to tear out the doughy inside before measuring out a *shmear* of lox spread. Mary grabbed the last cinnamon crunch bagel and slathered it with raisin walnut cream cheese.

On their way to a table on the far side of the room, Mary gushed, "That Al is kinda cute, huh?"

He's a bit chunky for me."

Mary licked her lips. "And what's so bad about a *chunky?*"

"You've got candy on the brain. It's a wonder you don't weigh two-hundred pounds."

Mary opened her mouth to respond, but was interrupted by the club's president. Sharon Rosen rapped on the podium.

A round of "shushing" preceded the members' welcoming the competent, organized woman at the helm with their applause. Everyone settled back in their seats, anxious to hear what their leader had to say.

"Quiet ladies," Sharon said, "we need to start on time. Another group has booked this room for a luncheon, so settle down. Just a reminder before we begin, mark your calendars. Annual membership dues are payable next month and you definitely don't want to miss that meeting. Our guest speaker will discuss Color Astrology—the new Feng Shui." Sharon cleared her throat. "This morning, author Lee Ravine will discuss her memoir, *Riding Solo: My Journey Through Love and Madness.* Lee holds degrees in Psychology and Special Education. When she's not volunteering at the Center for Living Well, she's busy working on her novel. It's my pleasure to introduce… Lee Ravine."

An enthusiastic round of applause subsided and a tall woman in her mid-seventies, her face framed by a mass of golden blond curls, made her way to the podium. She tugged at the neckline on her turquoise print blouse and adjusted her stylish eyewear before she spoke. "Good morning and thank you for your warm welcome." The author's gaze moved left-center-right. "I always knew that one day I'd write a book. I assumed it would be a memoir encompassing the first thirty-five years of my life. The fact that my family put a capital "D" in dysfunction may explain why I'm fascinated with all things psychological and feel comfortable around people with 'issues.'"

She shuffled her notes before continuing. "For much of my life, my goal was to be a psychotherapist and eventually earn my Ph.D. I was the go-to person whenever friends or co-workers struggled with personal problems. Their gratitude made my ego swell. In the end I came up short of my long-term goal. I'm sure many of you are aware that life is full of surprises."

Several of the women nodded.

For the next forty-five minutes the rapt audience listened as the author's journey, through love and lust, disillusionment and deceit, and ultimately survival, unfolded.

"My horrific ride on the merry-go-ride from hell is over. I stand before you… a survivor… a survivor of my journey through love and madness."

A member of the audience called out. "You never met *my* ex-husband."

"Or mine," another woman said.

Lee held up a copy of her book as if it were a trophy. "If you're looking for a memoir that reads like a novel and continues to receive five-star reviews, this is it. Thank you for inviting me here today and for being an attentive audience. I wish you all an easy journey."

Thunderous applause filled the room followed by a stimulating Q & A session and book signing.

TWENTY-SIX

PETER'S BUSINESS PARTNERSHIP with Stu left much to be desired. Responsibility for Villa Paraiso's day-to-day operation fell squarely on his shoulders and he resented breaking his ass for a fifty-fifty split. Stu rarely stopped by unless it was to pick up his share of money skimmed from operating expenses and kickbacks. If it wasn't for his competent assistant, Amy, Peter wasn't sure how he'd manage. He was fortunate to have this dedicated employee, a young single mother—and that she happened to be a hot piece of ass was an added perk.

Peter punched his intercom button. "Amy, I need you in here, Amy—"

Amy appeared in the office doorway, a pencil and pad clutched in her hand. "I can hear you. I'm not deaf, ya know."

"I'm on overload. So much to do around here and we still have to finalize plans for the July Fourth celebration."

Amy pursed her lips. "You sure it's not all that caffeine and sugar you've been guzzling?" She pointed to the tall coffee container in his hand. "Try staying away from that stuff."

Peter gulped down the remainder of his Grande Mocha Frappe Latte with extra syrup and whipped cream. Louis had insisted the Wi-Fi café include a barista to concoct creations with pretentious names. At first Peter protested, but after Louis' request turned into a demand, he gave in. Before long, he found himself addicted to the caffeinated beverages.

"How may I be of service?" Amy asked in a pseudo professional tone.

"Knock it off. I'm not in the mood."

Amy frowned. *I have a feeling this is going to be a long morning.*

Lately his pants had gotten tighter. Peter promised himself that once the party was over he'd take Amy's advice and cut back on the lattes.

TWENTY-SEVEN

PLANS FOR JULY 4TH were falling into place. Stu's contact at a local warehouse specialized in matching misplaced liquor shipments with interested parties, sort of like placing orphans with adoptive families. Local merchants offered to cater a portion of the food at a deep discount in exchange for placing their catering brochures on the tables. D.J. Mike, a local high school student, would provide music for a nominal fee, and the annual pyrotechnics display sponsored by the county rounded out the evening.

At precisely 7:00 p.m., D.J. Mike kicked off the party with a jazzed up version of *The Star-Spangled Banner*. Umbrella handles were decorated with red, white, and blue streamers. Small American flags on tables around the pool fluttered in the balmy breeze. Chicken and spareribs slathered with barbecue sauce sizzled on oversized portable grills alongside juicy hamburgers and foot-long hot dogs.

"These ribs are deeelicious," declared John Taylor. "Who says white men can't cook ribs?" He roared with laughter before he tore into his second helping of baby-backs.

His wife had been reluctant to attend the party, concerned John would embarrass them in front of what she referred to as "highfalutin white folk."

She shot him a withering glance. "Hush John, do you want someone to hear you?" She sniffed the air. "Phew! Something around here stinks."

"That's barbecue, baby. Mouth-watering, finger-lickin' good barbecue, what else?"

"I know damn-well what barbecue smells like and that sure as hell ain't barbecue. It's more likely road kill!"

John gave her a reproachful look. "Can't you just relax and enjoy yourself for a change?"

* * *

When John and Claudia had first visited the hospitality center, the sales staff couldn't have been nicer. John assured Claudia she'd feel comfortable living at Villa Paraiso, but she continued to grapple with social boundaries. She'd forever be that southern schoolgirl victimized by segregation. He understood where she was coming from, but it took great effort to ignore her obsession with what a black person should or shouldn't say, or how they should act if they find themselves in the minority.

John had earned a Ph.D. in Political Science and retired on a pension supplemented with wise investments. He didn't give a rat's ass what anybody thought about him. He'd served his country in Nam and was awarded a Bronze Star and a Purple Heart. He was reminded of his combat days whenever it rained. His left leg ached as a result of taking on shrapnel while engaged in combat, and the recurring nightmares, the horrible night terrors where he'd awaken angry enough to kill… again.

John spotted their neighbors searching for a place to sit. He jumped up and waived. "Jay! Beverly! There's plenty of room over here."

Claudia gave John a sharp nudge with her elbow. "There you go again."

"You betcha Mama," John said, "didn't you know this here table's the *Jim Crow Must Go* table?" John leaned over and swatted Claudia's ample hip.

She replied with a swift kick to his ankle.

"Damn you, girl. Mind your manners now," he whispered, welcoming Jay with a knuckle-bump and Beverly with a peck on the cheek.

By 9:30 p.m., satiated from the endless supply of food and alcoholic beverages and exhausted from twirling and twerking to D.J. Mike's throbbing rhythms, the crowd settled down for the main event.

The pool deck offered an unobstructed view of the crystal-clear sky illuminated by lights bursting in mid-air, a perfect ending to a perfect evening.

TWENTY-EIGHT

SHORTLY BEFORE DAWN, Hector pulled into the employee parking lot with the intention of washing his car. He popped the trunk and removed a bucket, sponge, and a bottle of detergent.

A moment earlier, he had been focused on the task at hand, but suddenly he felt distracted. He replaced the cleaning supplies back in the trunk, slammed the lid shut, and ran in the direction of where he'd last seen Charles and the *puta*.

A pungent odor filled his nostrils. He inched past a quagmire encircled with Bahia grass and observed an outline of a partially submerged form. Despite an egret perched serenely atop the inert object, his instinct warned that something was amiss.

Hector's feet felt as if they were riveted to the ground, but he willed himself to step closer. He parted the tall, coarse grass. A huge iguana whooshed past his leg. Hector slipped on spongy soil and leaped back. His arms flailed as he struggled to remain upright.

Still water rippled. The partially submerged form rotated ever so slightly. A human hand appeared above the waterline. Hector gasped as surging blood pounded in his ears. He imagined himself clenched between a ferocious beast's powerful jaws, his lifeless body dragged into the Reserve. He stumbled away blindly, as if besieged by demons.

Hector entered The Equator and lingered at the back of the room. He tugged at the ornate silver crucifix that hung from the chain around his neck. He prayed no one would notice his rapid breathing.

His co-workers were gathered in front of the podium. They shared stories about what they'd done over the weekend. Some of them had fished off local canals. Others hung around the house, guzzled beer and watched TV.

Hector was anxious to pick-up his work assignment and push the gory scene he'd stumbled upon from his mind. He tapped one of the men on the shoulder, "*¿Que pasa?*"

"Hey Hector, you okay? You don't look so good?"

"Jus' so stinkin' hot in here. Why you waitin'?"

"We waitin' on the boss. No boss, no work. The *gringo's* late for the first time in the history of the world. Maybe he's dead." The man's raspy laugh reverberated off the metal walls.

Hector's voice screamed inside his head, *Madre mia, dead!* Despite the thermometer on the wall that read ninety-four degrees, his hands felt ice cold.

One of the men called out, "Screw this shit, man, I ain't waitin' no more."

"You gonna go home for *siesta?*" another man shouted. Nervous laughter filled the room.

Always the voice of reason, Manny held up his hand. "*¡Silencio!*" He waited until the room went quiet. "If we hang around doin' nothin' we'll be in trouble for sure. If we look busy, we won't get in trouble. We can check back later. Maybe Farley will show up by then."

Manny motioned for the men to follow him outside. Within seconds, they had boarded their utility carts and headed off in different directions.

Hector hadn't noticed the mud he'd tracked inside until The Equator emptied out. In a panic, he pulled off his shoes and rinsed the soles in the washroom sink. He swept the residue into the parking lot and slammed the door behind him.

TWENTY-NINE

JOHN NAVIGATED THE WINDING ROAD leading to the clubhouse and for a moment imagined it to be a pewter-hued serpent lying in wait for unsuspecting prey. A local news helicopter banked and turned overhead. John felt as if he were back in 'Nam. Combat's indelible memories, saturated with napalm and discharged without regard for human life, seared his brain. In his mind, Ng stood before him, her delicate features and silken hair cascading over perfectly rounded breasts. He shuddered at her soothing touch, pleasure mixed with pain—the pain of leaving Ng, her swollen belly ripe with the fruit of their passion.

John was jolted back to reality when he pulled up under the clubhouse rotunda and the valet opened the car door.

"Morning, sir, wash today?"

"No thanks, maybe next time."

He exited the car and pointed in the direction of the noise overhead. "Any idea what that's all about?"

The valet slid behind the steering wheel. "Rumor has it, some dude's been murdered."

* * *

The Men's Club provided a refuge from wives and the forced togetherness, a byproduct of retirement. Not all wives were nagging shrews, but a few shared one minor fault. They never missed an opportunity to recite the ratio of calories to fat and point out the difference between good carbs and bad carbs.

Many of the members weren't interested in traditional retirement pursuits. They preferred instead the three "B's"—ball-breaking, bragging, and bullshitting—the foundation of any self-respecting men's organization. Most of these men had been hard-working businessmen or professionals, alpha males, used to taking charge and delegating responsibility. For most of their lives they'd focused on supporting their families and growing their retirement portfolio. No longer encumbered by obligations and deadlines, Villa Paraiso offered the opportunity to nurture mind, body and spirit.

John sat down in the vacant seat between Burt Rosen, the club's president, and a younger heavyset man he didn't recall seeing before. Across from them sat the impeccably dressed retired dentist rumored to be quite the ladies' man.

The men acknowledged John with a nod and returned to the daunting task of deciding which pastry to stuff into their mouths next, while Ed Marrone indulged them with exaggerated tales of pursuing dangerous criminals during his NYPD days.

John wondered if the valet knew what he was talking about. "Any idea why there's a TV chopper crisscrossing the property?"

A few of the men shrugged.

The hell with it, no one appears to be concerned, John thought, and headed for the refreshments set out on the sideboard.

An irresistible selection of pastries and muffins beckoned from huge platters decorated with paper doilies that seemed out of place in this testosterone-fueled environment. After much deliberation, he chose an almond croissant and a pastry topped with fresh raspberries. He poured a cup of black coffee and returned to the table.

"Hey, John," Burt said, "I'd like you to meet our new member, Al Frank."

John swallowed a bite of pastry and wiped his fingers on a napkin before holding out his hand. "Good to meet you."

"Same here," Al said.

"You chose a great place to live," John said. "It's more than that. It's a... a... lifestyle."

Al nodded. "You've got quite a grip. Ever play professional sports?"

At six feet, three inches tall, with a muscular build, John was often taken for a professional athlete. "A little college football."

A sudden gust of wind forced the bougainvilleas to beat against the building. The floor-to-ceiling windows shuddered followed by a flurry of activity outside. Sheriff's deputies ran back and forth and gestured wildly.

Ed stood up. "I'm going outside, the rest of you stay where you are."

"What do you mean *you're* going? We'll all go," shouted one of the men.

Ed rushed toward the exit. Members shoved each other and chairs toppled as they hurried to keep up.

Burt pounded his fist on the table in a futile attempt to regain order. A deputy sheriff pushed his way into the room. Burt shrugged apologetically. "Excuse me deputy. I'm Burt Rosen, president of the Men's Club. We're all anxious to know what the commotion's about."

"Is it true there's been a murder?" John asked.

"I can only confirm that a dead body's been reported to 9-1-1," the deputy said.

"So," John said, "the valet was right."

Al slapped his forehead. "I can't believe this. I thought I left this kinda crap back in New York."

Ed elbowed a few members, flipped open his wallet, and announced, "Retired NYPD."

"So what?" a voice called out.

"Shaddup asshole," Ed shouted over his shoulder. He directed himself to the deputy. "Anything I can do to help?"

The deputy frowned. "You can get everyone to line up with their photo ID out. I'll have a look-see and then they can all go home and stay put."

Ed felt pumped, like when he was on the job. "You heard the deputy. Now line up with your ID's in your hand and no shoving."

Tempers flared. Someone shouted, "Screw you, Ed!"

"Oh yeah, asshole?" Ed replied. "Screw you *and* the horse you rode in on."

THIRTY

FRESH FROM HER SHOWER, Vicky padded into the kitchen barefoot and continued to towel-dry her hair. She looked up, surprised to find Ed rummaging through the refrigerator. He lifted the orange juice carton to his lips and began to drink.

Vicky stepped forward. "What are you doing home?"

Startled, Ed spun around.

The container collided with Vicky's head. Juice spilled down the front of her silk, floral-print kimono and spattered onto the floor. "Look what you've done. I'm covered in juice."

"I'm sorry," Ed said, "but this has been one hell of a morning and I am pissed."

Vicky wiped the front of her kimono with the towel. "Weren't you supposed to be at a meeting?" She stooped down and blotted the floor.

"Do you have any idea what's going on out there?" Ed asked.

Vicky stood up, a blank expression on her face. "No, but I'm sure you'll tell me."

"Don't be such a wise-ass. More than thirty years on the force and I've been dissed and dismissed, like shit on the bottom of someone's shoe—"

"Knowing you, you probably stuck your nose where it doesn't belong." Vicky's tone softened. "Look, Ed, I know you're having a rough time adjusting to retirement, but I've been telling you, you need a hobby or something. Volunteer."

"You're the one person I expected to support me," Ed said. "I was demeaned. A helicopter almost blew in the clubhouse windows and the place is crawling with deputies. There's been a murder!"

"You're joking about the murder, right?"

Ed threw up his hands. "Yeah, it's a big joke, just like me." He turned and headed for the front door.

"Where are you off to now?"

"I need to clear my head."

Ed sped out of the driveway and almost clipped a cyclist entering the front gate. He continued west on Clint Moore and made a sharp right onto State Road 7. He floored the accelerator and blew through every yellow light and a couple of red ones.

The tension in his jaw subsided until he noticed the gas gauge was nearing empty. He pulled to a stop at a gas station adjacent to a bar and grill, removed a credit card from his wallet and exited the car.

A young black woman, wearing a crop-top, booty shorts and red patent-leather pumps with metallic toes and heels, paced back and forth and puffed on a cigarette. The moment she saw Ed, she disappeared around the side of the building.

Ed filled the gas tank and debated whether or not to get back in his car and drive off, or give in to his investigative instincts. He replaced the nozzle back on the pump and ducked his head around the corner of the building. Parked directly in front of him was the most incredible customized Monster truck, straight out of *American Truck Magazine*.

The Ford F350 Lariat crew cab, with a molten orange and black fiberglass shell, mounted on thirty-four-inch tires was impressive. Instead of the Ford logo, "Farley" was etched into custom caps attached to the shiniest rims imaginable. Mounted on the grill were steer horns, easily eight feet across and polished to a smooth marble finish.

Ed shook his head. "Sonofabitch. Farley's that guy Murph had the run-in with. What in hell is his truck doing here?"

Ed heard scraping coming from between the truck and the building. He ducked around the front of the truck and found the woman he had spotted out front cowering against the wall.

He flashed his gold NYPD detective's shield and hoped she wouldn't notice he wasn't from the Sheriff's Office. "Get over here."

The woman shook her head.

"Whaddaya mean *no?* Get the hell over here."

The woman stood up and moved closer.

"What's your name?" Ed asked.

No response.

"I'm not playing games here. What's your name?"

"Tulie, sir. Folks call me Tulie. It's my nickname, short for Tallulah."

"You'd better be telling the truth. I'll run you in if you're playin' me."

"No sir… I'm not lyin'. I know better than to lie to the lawman."

"What are you doing hanging out here?" Ed asked. "The joint's closed."

No response.

"I won't hesitate to take you in." Ed reached for handcuffs he no longer carried.

The woman flinched. "Been waitin' for Farley, don't know where he at."

"How long have you been here?"

"Umm… since Sunday night."

"Holy cow, you mean night before last?"

"Yeah, Farley don't never miss Sunday night."

"What have you been doing all this time?"

"Mostly waitin' and sleepin'." She pointed to the gas station's convenience store. "And snackin' some."

"Awfully long time to wait for someone."

Tulie lowered her voice. "Farley owes me money."

Ed nodded. "Isn't there anyone waiting on you, wondering where the hell you are?"

"No sir. I only got my son and my mom's at home and I called her. She ain't worried none. Told her I was workin' a double shift."

"You said Farley never missed a Sunday night, how come?"

"Well, that's Sand Dune's special night, ya know."

"No, I don't know. What's so special about Sunday?"

"Oreo night."

"What the hell is Oreo night? Oh… I get it. That's when good ol' boys snack on sweet brown sugar."

Tulie put her hands on her hips and stamped her foot. "I'm Farley's gal."

"If you're Farley's gal how'd you end up out here?"

Tulie stared at the ground. "Farley was drinkin' with this guy I ain't never seen before. Mostly Farley's alone, but sometimes he be bringin' a friend to party. I remember thinkin' I sure hope this guy ain't part of the deal."

"So tell me, *Farley's gal,* this guy… what'd he look like?"

"Mean lookin' S.O.B., kinda short, mustache, nasty puss-ugly nose. Could be Mexican."

"Go on."

"Guy's a mess, snortin' coke, drinkin' too much. Kept wipin' his face with a faded bandana."

"And you? Were you snorting shit too?"

Tulie shook her head. "No sir, not me. I seen what it do. Drinkin' and laughin', a little dancin', that's what Tulie's all about."

"And makin' a buck?"

"Well, that too."

"So the last time you laid eyes on Farley's drunk ass it was hanging off a barstool?"

"No sir. He walked me out to his truck and told me to wait for him. I had a feelin' the two of them had some business goin' on. I wasn't lookin' for no ass-whuppin' so I didn't ask no questions."

"Got any ID?" Ed asked. "I need to know where to find you if I have any more questions."

Tulie rummaged through her handbag until she found her driver's license. She handed it to Ed.

He took note of the address, a run-down public housing complex often featured on the local news.

"I have a hunch Farley won't be here anytime soon. Need a ride?"

"No, sir. I'm waitin' on a friend."

Ed reached out and ran his hand across the truck's grill. *One abandoned truck, one missing Farley, and a dead body back at Villa Paraiso. This has got to be the mother lode.*

As Ed turned to leave, Tulie tugged at his sleeve. "Please sir, don't tell nobody 'bout how Tulie gets her money... don't want my little boy knowin'."

THIRTY-ONE

A PROFUSION OF STROBE LIGHTS mounted atop two police cruisers, accompanied by death's unmistakable stench, announced trouble up ahead.

As he approached the grizzly crime scene, perspiration pooled on Detective Daniels' shiny bald head, trickled down his neck, and saturated what had been a freshly laundered shirt earlier that morning. In all his years with the Sheriff's Office he'd never gotten used to *leftovers* exposed to the elements. He lifted the yellow crime scene tape and suppressed the urge to wretch.

Deputy Taylor approached. "Okeydokey," Taylor said, "got it all under control. Area's cordoned off and detour stanchions are in place on the internal roadway. M.E.'s on her way."

"Good," Daniels said. "Sheriff will have our asses if we screw this one up." *Damn murder has to be in an uppity-up gated community.*

Both men moved closer to the edge of the pond.

Daniels barked orders into his two-way radio. "Make sure you techs don't compromise any of my evidence. Better make damn well sure you've got something worthwhile before you drop those markers like bread crumbs."

Taylor pointed to the partially submerged body. "Maybe

if we're lucky we'll find a wallet on him. Don't suppose he worked here?"

"From the appearance of the clothing and shoes, that's a possibility."

Taylor nodded. "Anyhow, M.E.'s gotta take a look before we get the okay to dredge the pond."

"When do you think that'll be?"

Taylor shrugged. "We're waitin' on the equipment now. Sure hope she gets here soon. Torso appears to be intact, but the poor guy came close to having his head decapitated. Could be the murder weapon's a chain saw."

"Damn head better stay connected even if it's hanging by a thread. Has management been notified?"

"Took care of that first thing," Taylor said. "Say, do you think they'll get any decent prints off the corpse?"

"Depends on how waterlogged the fingers are and if the maggots haven't gotten to them. Might need to slice 'em before they roll 'em and print 'em."

Taylor grimaced. "Glad I'm not the one doin' it."

A stocky, clean-shaven man in his late fifties, wearing a tan silk shirt, slacks, and matching Docksiders, hurried in the direction of Daniels and Taylor. He shielded the sun's glare with his hand. "I'm Property Manager Peter Duke," he said. "I was offsite and rushed over as soon as I got the call from my assistant."

Daniels removed his sunglasses and mopped his brow with a handkerchief before the two men shook hands.

"I'd like to see the body if that's okay with you," Peter said.

"Sorry, that's not possible 'til after we get the go-ahead."

"Do you know who found the body and called it in?"

"Dispatch reported the message was garbled, but the caller sounded Latino."

"If I were you," Peter said, "I'd start the questioning with the maintenance crew."

"Are they the only ones around here who speak with a Spanish accent? For all we know the caller is one of your residents."

"I just figured it's the logical place to start."

Daniels resented Peter telling him how to do his job, but his suggestion made sense. "Go ahead, round up your crew," Daniels said. "Let me know when they're all in one place and I'll have a go at 'em." He rattled off his cell number, clicked on his two-way radio, and continued to bark orders.

Peter stored Daniels' number in his iPhone before calling the maintenance extension. The phone rang for a full minute. He knew Farley's reputation for hitting the sauce hard. *Lazy, redneck, bastard. He's probably sleeping off a bender. I'll rip him a new one when I see him.*

Peter headed in the direction of the maintenance building. He wasn't used to running around in sweltering heat and the unanswered phone call intensified his discomfort. He blew through the door prepared to tear into Farley and was surprised to find maintenance workers leaning against walls or sitting on the concrete floor nodding off. He unleashed his frustration on them instead. "What in hell is going on here? Where's your boss?"

Several of the men, their eyes cast downward, shifted their weight from one foot to the other, but no one dared to speak.

"We have a damn emergency here!" Peter yelled. "If I don't get some cooperation I'll fire the whole lot of you. You can go back to wherever the hell you came from and I'll hire another shitload of wetbacks to replace you, *comprende?*"

One of the men called out, *"Sí... sí..."* we here to work, but no Farley, no work orders."

Peter's eyes scanned the room. "This can't be all of you. Get out there and spread the word. We need everybody to report back here, *pronto!"*

Peter stood in the center of the prefab structure and assessed the rusted lockers, second-hand refrigerator for storing bag lunches, and half a dozen low wooden stools. The grossly inadequate ceiling fans and absence of air-conditioning or a water cooler compounded the deplorable conditions. *Can't do anything about it now, he thought, but if I don't want to die of heat-stroke, I'd better phone Daniels and tell him the meeting's in the clubhouse.*

Peter pulled a sheet of paper from the clipboard hanging on the side of the makeshift podium and printed in large block letters:

ATTENCIÓN
MAINTENANCE MEETING
PRONTO! AQUÍ!
CLUBHOUSE – VERANDA ROOM

He pulled two Band-Aids from a half-empty container perched on a windowsill and attached the notice securely to the front door.

On his way to the clubhouse, he grappled with how to break the news to Louis and Stu. *How the hell am I going to explain that a murder happened on my watch?*

THIRTY-TWO

THE ODOR OF STALE CIGARETTE SMOKE mixed with sweat wafted across the Veranda Room. The maintenance crew, still wearing their Day-Glow reflective vests, whispered to one another, "Why we here? They roundin' up illegals?"

Peter Duke paced back and forth at the front of the room. He regretted not stopping at his office to change out of his soiled shirt and grass-stained slacks. Anxious for Daniels to arrive, he glanced at the doorway and checked his watch every few minutes.

Hector folded his arms across his chest, closed his eyes, and rocked back-and-forth in his seat. *My stinkin' ID better be good as gringo who sold it to me promised.*

A hand brushed his arm. He flinched. Seated next to him, a woman from housekeeping tugged at her skirt.

"I didn't mean to startle you," the woman, Rosa, said. She pointed to a portion of the skirt pinned under Hector's thigh. He moved his leg to release the material and mumbled an apology. The woman's warm smile reminded him of his mother.

Detective Daniels entered the Veranda Room flanked by four forensic technicians pushing squeaking carts loaded with evidence kits and folding screens. Daniels examined the curious faces as he took long strides toward the front of the room. Lots of possibilities here. Murderer could be any one of them, or not.

"I'd almost given up on you," Peter said.

"Had to wait for the M.E. and this equipment to arrive. Can't begin an interrogation without it."

"Can I give you a hand with anything?"

"No thanks. Techs are setting up in each corner of the room. Won't be long now before they're ready."

"Good, good. While I was waiting for you, I thought of something."

"Yeah, what's that?"

"My maintenance supervisor's a hard-ass, rules with an iron hand. No one dares to step out of line or disobey him. Made more than a few enemies along the way, but he doesn't strike me as someone who would abandon his post unless he's dead-drunk or just plain dead."

"We'll know soon enough," Daniels said. He turned his attention to the bustle of activity around the room's perimeter and frowned. "C'mon… c'mon, times a wastin'. What's the holdup?"

One of the techs called out, "Just a few more minutes."

Daniels addressed the restless group, "Okay people, listen up. I'm Detective Daniels and I'll be heading up this investigation. If you haven't already heard, this gathering's about a murder." He allowed a few seconds for his words to sink in. He stared menacingly and pointed a finger at his restless audience.

"You're all suspects," he snarled. "You *will* cooperate with the Palm Beach County Sheriff's Office in every way possible, got that? So, sit tight, because we're gonna be here for quite some time unless one of you confesses right now and saves us a heap of trouble."

Rosa stood and approached one of the two deputies stationed at the door in the back of the room.

Hector's heart skipped a beat. *She reportin' me actin' weird.* He felt relieved when he saw the female deputy nod and Rosa crossed the hall to the women's bathroom.

Manny plopped down in the vacant chair next to Hector and whispered, "A murder here? *¡Ay, Díos Mio!* Can you believe it?"

No reply.

Manny cuffed Hector on the back of the head. "Didn't you hear me, you deaf or somethin'?"

"Uh-uh, jus keep your voice down."

"Hector, you're actin' wacko, man. What the hell is with you?"

Hector remained silent.

Manny stifled a laugh, "Between the prowler and the murder, no tellin' who's runnin' around out there."

"Shut up Manny or—"

"Or what, you gonna kill me?" He tousled Hector's hair and returned to his seat a few rows back.

Rosa re-entered the Veranda Room franticly waiving her hand.

Daniels addressed the petite woman. "Are we about to hear a confession from the little lady back there?"

Rosa marched to within inches of Daniels' chest. "In this room I see maintenance workers, no one else. Is one of our own dead, is that why we are here?"

Daniels snickered, "You're a sharp little gal, ain't ya? Maybe when this is over you can apply for my job."

"Because I'm a woman, I'm not smart... not educated? I clean people's dirt, but that doesn't make me less worthy."

"Let me tell you people something," Daniels said. "One of the first things we look for in a murder investigation is who benefits most from the crime. Since the man you all love to hate's whereabouts are unknown and what happened here isn't a murder, it's a goddamned mutilation, there's a good possibility the victim's your boss Farley."

Gasps echoed throughout the room followed by high-fives. The maintenance crew made no secret about their festering hostility.

THIRTY-THREE

REBECCA'S DAUGHTER AND SON-IN-LAW had arrived at her Bronx apartment with a U-Haul hitched to the back of their car. They'd helped her sort through a lifetime of memories before the Salvation Army truck hauled away what was left. Rebecca had had no choice but to comply, even though she doubted that the New York City Housing Authority had condemned her apartment building. She was convinced her daughter was in cahoots with Peter Duke.

* * *

Despite living with her daughter and son-in-law for the past six months, Rebecca refused to avail herself of Villa Paraiso's amenities. She preferred to sit alone at the breakfast counter in a kitchen larger than her old apartment. She thumbed through Miriam's magazines featuring painfully thin women she was certain would benefit from an infusion of brisket.

Rebecca often prepared her own meals. Miriam and Aaron no longer served the traditional foods she was accustomed to. They preferred *traif,* the non-Kosher food served in the clubhouse. Miriam had asked her mother to join her and Aaron for lunch, but as usual she declined their invitation.

The whirring in the distance didn't concern Rebecca until the helicopter hovered directly overhead. The noise was deafening. She was forced to cover her ears and feared the rotors would graze the rooftop and the ceiling would rain down on her head. She grabbed the phone with trembling hands and called her daughter's cell number.

"Mom," Miriam said, "is everything all right?"

"Yes, yes, but I changed my mind about lunch."

Miriam covered the phone with her hand. "It's mother. She'd like to join us for lunch."

"Now?" Aaron said. "I'm almost finished with my coffee."

Miriam frowned. "She doesn't sound like herself, something must have spooked her."

"Mom, are you there?"

"Nu, where else would I be?"

"Aaron will pick you up in a few minutes… and mom, please wear something nice."

"Vu den, I should come to your clubhouse in a *shmatta?"*

Rebecca slammed down the phone. Hot tears splattered the countertop. She wiped the cool granite with her elbow. *God forbid I should stain the surface. They need such a kitchen, for what, to boil water? I hate it here. I miss my facockta apartment, the cold radiators… ech, even the cockroaches.*

Rebecca hurried to the guest bedroom to change into something "nice," but vowed not to eat one morsel of *goyishe* food.

* * *

Miriam was delighted her mother had given in and emerged from self-imposed isolation. Aaron drummed his fingers on the table and stared into his third cup of coffee. Rebecca ordered a plain bagel with a *shmear* of cream cheese, but a plain bagel wasn't included in the selection offered.

"Sorry ma'am," the server said. "May I suggest blueberry, organic honey-wheat, sundried tomato, or sunflower seed?"

"Nisht gut," Rebecca said. "For this I put on something nice?"

"Ma."

Rebecca shrugged. "This…" She pointed to the menu. "How do you say it?"

"Ma'am, Croissant."

"I'll try it and I'll take a glass of hot tea."

"Ma'am, a glass?"

"Oy! Yes, a glass." She turned toward Miriam. "I'm never coming here again. From now on I stay where I belong. I wear my old bloomers and eat what I want, and *dus is alas.* That's it."

Just then, a pleasant looking couple approached. Aaron pushed back his chair and rose to greet them. Rebecca seized the opportunity to leave the table. "I'm going to the bathroom."

"I'll come with you, Ma."

"You stay," she said. "Some things I can still do by myself."

Rebecca stepped into the corridor. Two deputies passed her and entered the Veranda Room across the hall. Before the door closed, she observed a group of grungy-looking men and a few women seated in long rows. Two men stood talking to each other at the front of the room.

A gasp caught in her throat. She thought she recognized one of them. She yanked open the door and marched down the aisle. Standing face-to-face with her old slumlord, Peter Duke, Rebecca suddenly felt dizzy. She grasped a chair for support.

Peter tried to recall where he had seen the elderly woman before, her stooped posture and look of despair seemed familiar.

Daniels reached out and touched Rebecca's elbow. "Ma'am, can I help you? This is a private meeting. Are you lost?"

She turned and glared at Peter.

A glimmer of recognition crossed his face. "Mrs. Ehrlich, isn't it? What a surprise. I never expected to see you here."

Hearing Peter's voice evoked powerful emotions. Rebecca bent over, yanked off her orthopedic shoe, and hit Peter. *Whap!* "You... you no good *momsa*. You're worse than a murderer." *Whap! Whap!*

The confused onlookers strained to get a better look at the drama unfolding at the front of the room. They whispered to each other excitedly and a few attempted to leave. Deputies ushered them back to their seats. Daniels grabbed the fleshy part of Rebecca's arm, wrestled the shoe from her hand and pointed it at Rosa. "You tell them in Spanish to settle down and nobody leave until I say so."

Rosa repeated the directive in Spanish and then in English.

Daniels didn't realize he had exerted excessive force to restrain Rebecca until she squealed in pain. He released his grip on her arm. "Are you nuts, lady? Don't you realize I can arrest you for what you just did?"

"That bastard deserves to be punished for what *he* did to me."

Daniels imagined this elderly woman was reacting to an injustice, real or imagined, but Peter Duke *worse* than a murderer? *Is that possible?* Daniels shifted his gaze from Rebecca to the commotion at the entrance just in time to see Peter exit the room and a visibly agitated woman enter. She rushed toward the front of the room.

"Mom, I've been looking all over for you. What are you doing in here?"

For Christ's sake, what now, another crazy gal? Daniels massaged his temples. *This is going to be one hell of a day, for sure.*

Miriam stopped to catch her breath and was shocked to see her mother's tear-stained face and the welt she kneaded on her upper arm. She scowled. "What have you done to my mother? Look at her arm. She's a defenseless old lady. What did she do to warrant this abuse?"

Before Daniels had a chance to reply, Miriam pulled her mother close and hugged her. "Ma, it's all my fault. I never should have forced you to come to live with us."

The old woman's face brightened. *My tuchta thinks I'm an old fool, but stupid I'm not. I knew it. She lied to me. My building wasn't condemned.*

"Please, can my mother go now? I'm sure this is a misunderstanding."

Daniels gestured toward the door. "I'll let her go if you promise to keep a close watch on her."

"I promise."

Rebecca poked Daniels' chest. "You should make my *tuchta* promise not to *schlep* me around like a sack of rags."

"Please, Ma, enough already. Let's just get out of here."

Daniels hadn't eaten breakfast and his head felt as if it were about to explode. He instructed a deputy to escort the two women outside and round up an egg sandwich, a large container of black coffee, and a couple of aspirins.

THIRTY-FOUR

PETER HUSTLED DOWN THE CORRIDOR toward his office. *What are the odds that I'd run into one of my old tenants, a million-to-one?*

He unbuttoned his shirt and rushed past his assistant, Amy.

She stopped rifling through a file tray overflowing with folders and followed Peter into his private office.

He kicked off his loafers, removed his belt, and unzipped his pants.

She pulled off her blouse and stepped out of her skirt.

Peter turned to find Amy standing in the middle of the room bathed in sunlight, wearing nothing more than a lace bra and matching silk panties.

"What the hell are you doing?" he asked.

"I… I thought… I don't know what I thought."

"You're like Pavlov's dog. You hear a man's zipper and it's time to screw."

"That's a nasty thing to say. You know that's not true."

The murder and bumping into one of his old tenants had upset Peter more than he realized. He had lashed out at Amy with cruel words he wished he could take back. She didn't deserve to be denigrated. She was much more than his assistant. Amy had proven herself to be a loyal employee, his confidant and a caring, passionate lover.

He locked the office door, unfurled the Roman window shades and held out his arms.

Amy hesitated.

"I'm sorry. Come… please," he said in a hoarse voice.

She stepped forward, nuzzled his chest and tugged at his briefs. He hooked his thumbs onto her panties and rolled them down her thighs, kneaded her buttocks, and nibbled her ear. He murmured sentiments that until now had gone unspoken.

THIRTY-FIVE

HECTOR WOULD HAVE PREFERRED to sit quietly until it was his turn to be questioned, but with Rosa seated next to him he found it impossible to ignore her.

"My Aunt Maggie came to this country as a young woman," Rosa said. "She worked two jobs to save enough money to open Café Cantina." She lowered her voice. "Manny is her special customer. Whenever he comes in she stops whatever she's doing to serve him heaping plates of food."

"He lucky man."

"Manny introduced me to Farley. He offered me part-time work and suggested I clean for residents on my days off. It is against management's policy, but he promised not to tell if I paid him a weekly commission in cash."

Hector nodded. *She one smart lady. In America, speak good English mean everything. I try think good English, speak good English, maybe get two jobs.* He dozed off whenever there was a lull in the conversation. Each time he opened his eyes he saw Rosa smiling at him.

A deputy directed Hector to a screened area on the far side of the room.

His mind raced. *I don' know nothin'. I no kill nobody.*

He took a deep breath and entered the area behind the screen, where a stern-looking female investigator waited.

She glanced at Hector's driver's license and employee ID and asked the questions she had repeated throughout the afternoon. She jotted down his responses before moving on to collect physical evidence, her slender fingers sheathed in latex gloves. She painstakingly inspected the soles of his work shoes, clothing, hands and nails, and carefully placed scrapings, swabs, and strips of tape in evidence collection bags.

By 5:40 p.m., the last of the employees had been processed and the hungry, weary suspects were told they were free to leave. They offered an audible sigh of relief as they filed out of the room.

Rosa invited Hector to join her for dinner at her Aunt Maggie's restaurant.

Hector's stomach rumbled. "I... I like to come, but..." He patted his pants pocket. I have little money."

"No need for money. You are my guest."

"I am pleased to join you, but I will need directions."

A self-satisfied smile crossed Rosa's lips. *"No hay problema.* Just follow my car."

THIRTY-SIX

A PUBLIC RELATIONS nightmare ensued following Farley's brutal murder. Bone-chilling details appeared in newspapers from coast to coast.

The last of Phase II's unsold inventory and a disgruntled sales staff were a constant reminder that despite beefed-up security, the murder hung over Villa Paraiso like a shroud. Half-a dozen maintenance workers had flown the coop without picking up their last paycheck. Peter expected their remaining co-workers to pick-up the slack.

He promoted Manny to interim maintenance supervisor at a considerably lower salary than Farley had earned and made it clear the promotion was temporary. He planned to pocket the difference and take his time in hiring a permanent replacement, a win-win situation all around.

Residents questioned whether or not a connection existed between the prowler and Farley's murder, and single women were reluctant to venture out alone at night. The local spy store's entire stock of mace spray and police whistles had sold out the day after the murder.

Rumors spread like wildfire. Depending on each person's version of the event, the prowler was described as a tall, dark-skinned man or a short, fat, Caucasian, and everything in-between. Varying accounts had him carrying a baseball bat, a tire iron, or a tree limb.

Peter received numerous phone calls from residents demanding to know the steps he had taken to protect them from the now eight-foot tall monster with enormous fangs, brandishing a flaming torch in one hand and a machete in the other.

In an attempt to assuage their fears, Peter set up a robo-call informing everyone that the situation was under control. He hoped the message would sound convincing even though the son-of-a-bitch might still be out there.

Morale was at an all-time low. Peter needed to come up with an event to take everyone's mind off the tragedy and restore the serenity promised in Villa Paraiso's sales brochure. He and Amy considered several possibilities before calling the clubhouse caterer.

Colorful flyers were distributed to each villa announcing a South of the Border Fiesta complete with authentic music, food, and drink.

THIRTY-SEVEN

THE DAYS THAT FOLLOWED produced a whirlwind of activity in preparation for the upcoming event. Peter had stopped taking phone calls unless they were urgent or had something to do with the fiesta.

Amy insisted that he take one call.

"How many times do I have to tell you?" he said. "No phone calls! Do you have shit for brains?"

Amy disregarded the outburst and instead chose to recall their passionate lovemaking the day Farley's body was discovered.

Peter had conveniently forgotten to phone Louis with news of the murder, but now the nutcase was on the line.

"How could you keep me in the dark about something this important?" Louis said. "I had to hear about it from a player at a Las Vegas craps table? Lucky for me, I'd tossed the dice and made my point or I would've lost my concentration or worse, the contents of my stomach."

"I've been under a lot of pressure," Peter said. "I wasn't thinking straight."

"You're under pressure? What about me?"

"I didn't want to worry you unnecessarily. I wanted to wait—"

"Wait! Wait for what? I trusted you and Stu to handle everything and look what happened. Jeez, I can't believe we're discussing a... a... I can't even say the word. How bad is it over there?"

"Compared to what?"

"Not funny."

"Just how bad did your source say it is?"

"For Christ's sake, your guy was mutilated! Anyhow, day after tomorrow I'm taking Southwest flight 3049 arriving in Fort Lauderdale at 4:25 p.m., and you better make damn sure you're there on time to pick me up."

The line went dead.

Dealing with Louis long-distance was difficult enough. Peter dreaded the unpleasant scene that would surely play out at the airport.

He had little patience for the nutcase when he was off his head meds, but Louis was the money man and without him Villa Paraiso wouldn't exist. Peter would be back up north freezing his ass off and collecting rents from deadbeats, drug dealers, and little old ladies.

THIRTY-EIGHT

LOUIS' FLIGHT WAS SCHEDULED to arrive on the day of the fiesta and Peter didn't have time to hang out at the cell phone lot. Before 9/11, he would have handed the uniformed traffic agent a couple of bucks and parked outside the baggage claim area. He decided to give it a try, but was waived off and directed to the parking garage.

Inside the terminal, Louis paced in front of an empty baggage carousel and chewed the inside of his cheek. He unleashed a barrage of expletives the moment he spotted Peter. "Can you believe this shit?" he said. "We landed fifteen fuckin' minutes ago and I'm still waiting for my goddamned bag."

Peter recalled that Louis had often explained away his outbursts as a lack of impulse control. *Impulse control, my ass,* Peter thought. *What he needs is a good kick in the ass.*

"I'm friggin jet-lagged. I need to crash for a couple of hours."

"Okay. I'll drop you off at the hotel and you can—"

"I've wasted enough time."

"Well, there's a couch in my office."

"That'll do."

Louis was too self-absorbed to notice that he'd been

waiting in the wrong place all along. He continued his meltdown until they located the correct baggage claim area.

A blaring klaxon alerted the weary passengers to the arrival of baggage from flight 3049. The carousel completed a second revolution before Louis spotted his bag. He emitted a shrill "Whoopee!" before yanking the bag off the carousel. He extended the handle and rushed past Peter toward the revolving door. In the short span of a few minutes Louis' mood had fluctuated from a raging emotional maelstrom to that of a gleeful child.

During the ride back to Boca, Peter kept conversation to a minimum. As the car exited the turnpike, he glanced over at his passenger. Louis had nodded off.

With any luck he'll continue his nap on my couch, Peter thought. *Hopefully, if he's well rested he'll act normal this evening… if that's even possible.*

THIRTY-NINE

VILLA PARAISO'S FOOD AND BEVERAGE manager had worked his tail off to put together an incredible event. He transformed *La Plaza* into a bustling fiesta complete with a life-size *papier mâché* donkey. *Piñatas* hung from the ceiling and colorful fringed blankets decorated serving stations. Off to the side of the room Sangria cascaded down a three-tiered, stainless-steel fountain.

The maintenance crew appreciated the opportunity to earn a few extra dollars serving and cleaning up inside the air-conditioned clubhouse. They dressed in festive native costumes. The men wore over-sized sombreros and vests decorated with metallic threads and the women wore ruffled skirts and embroidered blouses.

At first, Hector had second thoughts about signing on for this optional assignment until he caught sight of Rosa. For a moment he forgot his discomfort, the ill-fitting costume, and scratchy fake mustache.

The guests filled their plates with sizzling fajitas, enchiladas, and tortillas filled with chicken or beef, tacos piled high with crisp cabbage, avocado, cheese and salsa. The array of mouth-watering foods continued on the opposite side of the room with roasted ears of corn, rice cooked with chilies and tomatoes, and steaming bowls of black beans.

At one serving station, adorned with a Mexican flag, the tantalizing aroma of *mole pablano,* Mexico's national dish, beckoned. Chicken and chocolate melded together produced a fiery sweet concoction that proved impossible to resist.

A strolling mariachi band, dressed in *charro* suits trimmed with gold braid, serenaded the crowd. The revelers signaled their approval with plastic cups filled with Sangria held high.

FORTY

ED HAD BEGGED VICKY to skip her weekly card game and accompany him to the fiesta.

"I don't wanna disappoint the girls," she'd said. "I'll meetcha later and don't forget to save me a seat near the food."

Vicky patted her expanding muffin-top. She had given up trying to shed a few pounds. Between menopause and eating out, all attempts to lose weight had failed miserably. Jogging didn't seem to help, not when she was distracted by clandestine liaisons. Besides, Ed loved her unconditionally; he'd told her so each time he apologized for his impotence. She didn't have the heart to tell him she was still the same lusty broad he busted in Times Square. Love wasn't enough.

She had arranged to leave the card game early in order to meet-up with her lover. She didn't delude herself into thinking these stolen moments were anything more than a service rendered, not unlike Charles' dance lessons. The brief encounters satisfied her longing for the passionate sex she craved and the intimacy Ed no longer provided.

* * *

Vicky lingered in the doorway and scanned the crowd,

hoping to see Ed. She was unaware that Charles had followed her inside until he brushed his hand across her butt. She turned and glared at him before she hurried inside.

Mary gawked. "I don't believe what I just saw."

The other women at the table twisted in their seats straining to catch a glimpse of whatever had caught Mary's attention.

"Damn," Mary said, "you missed it."

"Missed what? What are you talking about?" Jane asked.

"Mind telling the rest of us what's going on?" another woman asked.

"Who'da thunk it?" Mary said. "Sadie Sadie married lady waltzes in here with—of all people—Charles, the dance *teacha*," Mary said.

Eleanor and her sister stared at each other in amazement. "Isn't he gay?"

Beth chimed in, "It's none of our business who Charles sleeps with or whether he's gay or straight."

The other women at the table were on her like a pack of wild dogs.

"Of course it's our business," they yapped.

"We have a right to know everything about him," Beth said. "He *is* an employee."

Angela interrupted, "Ladies, you should hear how you sound. Meow! Meow! Meow! I don't understand why it's so important to have a man in your life."

Mary pointed toward the ceiling. "Hah! Didn't you devote yourself to *that* man for a good part of *your* life?"

Angela's face burned. *Living here is like living in a fishbowl.*

The mariachi band circled the table and made it impossible for the women to continue their conversation. They craned their necks in an attempt to catch a glimpse of Vicky and Charles, but the couple had moved off in different directions and blended into the crowd.

FORTY-ONE

ON HIS WAY TO THE FIESTA, Ed decided to stop by and shoot the breeze with the guards on break. He descended the staircase at the rear of the clubhouse lobby two steps at a time and rounded the corner. Raucous laughter erupted from inside the security office, located next to the administrative offices, at the end of the corridor.

Ed knocked before he pushed the unlocked door open.

The barrel-chested Chief of Security, Murph, struggled to his feet. He ambled over to Ed and the two men shook hands. "Good to see you, Ed."

"Good to see you too. Hey, you may want to keep it down a little. Don't want management to think you're having too much fun on the job."

"Hell, I didn't realize we're making that much noise." Murph turned to the two guards seated on the couch. "You know Ed Marrone don't you?"

"Sure do," Bill, the older man, said and reached over to shake Ed's hand.

The younger man nodded.

"Sounds like you're having your own private party down here. How come I wasn't invited?"

"You know you're welcome anytime," Murph said. "Now

that you're here, you'll get a kick out of this sex-mobile story."

"Sex-mobile?"

Another round of raucous laughter erupted. The Chief coughed up a phlegm plug the size of a cherry and spit it into the waste paper basket. He held up his hand to quiet the other men.

Scottie, the younger guard with the shaved head and a blanket of tattoos covering his forearms, cleared his throat. "We were talkin' about the 'you call-we deliver service'." He shielded his mouth with his hand and lowered his voice. "You should see the hot lookin' chicks that deliver, and I don't mean Chinese take-out."

"I get the picture," Ed said. "How often does this happen?"

Bill's Adam's-apple bobbed up and down as he spoke. "It's a regular Friday night event. A resident calls the gate and it's not long before a black Town Car with tinted windows shows up. There are always two women sitting in the back seat wearing huge grins and not much else."

"You talking three-ways here?" Ed asked.

The Chief shook his head. "Nah. We did a little surveillance and it looks like four men are sharing the two gals. The driver shuttles them around. Each female makes two stops and stays about fifteen minutes each time. After an hour or so, they're outta here."

"Not much you can do about it," Ed said.

The older guard shrugged.

"Not my style," Scottie said. "Personally, I hate sloppy seconds."

"See all the fun you're missing around here," the Chief said. "You oughta stop by more often. By the way, what brings you down here this evening?"

"Just wanted to find out if there's anything's new on the murder investigation."

"Matter of fact, there is," Murph said. "My source tells me Sheriff's Office is cock-sure one of Villa Paraiso's very own did the deed, but I betcha they'd have wrapped this up a lot sooner with you sniffin' around."

"I appreciate your vote of confidence. Maybe I'll do a little sniffing at tonight's shindig."

"Have yourself a good time and hoist a glass for me," Murph said.

"Thanks, I'll be sure and do that."

* * *

Ed entered the party room and spotted Peter Duke standing alongside a man he didn't recognize. He watched as Peter scooped spoons filled with *mole pablano* onto his plate. The concoction reminded Ed of something he had seen oozing from a corpse back when he was on the job.

He'd been waiting for the right moment to share the information he'd obtained during his encounter with Tulie and this was that moment. "I hear Villa Paraiso's taking all the heat for the murder."

Peter paused, the spoon in mid-air. "Where'd you hear that?"

Ed ignored the question. "What if I told you I have information that would put a new spin on the murder investigation?"

Peter arched his eyebrow. "Go on, I'm listening."

"From what I understand," Ed said, "the Sheriff's Office has been focusing on your employees to the exclusion of anyone outside the community."

"Maybe. Maybe not," Peter said.

Louis had been standing nearby gnawing on the inside of his cheek. "You wake me up for a damn party and now this clown's bugging us," Louis whined. "Who the hell is this guy?"

"Take it easy, Louis."

Peter turned his attention back to Ed. "You're that retired cop aren't you?"

"NYPD detective first-grade Edward Marrone at your service."

Louis glowered at Ed. "We don't care who you are. If you've got something to say, spit it out."

"This isn't the best place for us to talk," Peter said.

Louis stamped his foot like a petulant child. "This is as good a place as any, 'cause you're not dragging me anywhere else tonight."

"Peter's right," Ed said. "It's too damn noisy in here."

Peter put down his plate and reached out to guide Louis toward the caterer's pantry.

Louis yanked his arm away. "I don't need your help."

Peter crossed the room and pushed through the swinging door hidden from view behind a decorated folding screen. Louis reluctantly trailed behind. Ed followed.

It didn't take more than a few minutes before a loud argument erupted from inside the pantry.

At that exact moment, Hector stepped in front of the pantry door holding an empty chafing dish. Suddenly, the door swung open and Ed and Louis tumbled into the party room knocking Hector to the floor.

Hector scrambled to his feet and rubbed his bruised arm. He tore off the false mustache and flung his sombrero across the room before he darted toward the exit.

Rosa stood off to the side, a reproachful expression etched in her face. This complicated man had entered her life at a time when she had given up on her dream of finding true love. She wondered if she had opened her heart to disappointment.

Ed and Louis continued to tussle until Peter pulled them apart, but not before he'd dodged a roundhouse punch thrown by Louis. The two men released their grip on each other and stood in the center of the room panting.

"Simmer down and follow me back to my office," Peter said, before he turned and addressed the stunned onlookers. "Sorry for the interruption, folks. It's part of the entertainment. Enjoy the rest of your evening."

Security guards hurried across the floor, but Peter waved them off. "Everything's under control. My buddies here had too much to drink."

On his way out, Peter glanced at the Mexican flag's bold colors. Green represented hope, white purity, and red union—qualities Villa Paraiso no longer possessed.

FORTY-TWO

PETER TURNED ON THE LIGHTS in his office and walked over to the portable bar set up against one wall. Ed plopped down in an armchair and Louis slouched on the couch. Peter poured three shots of Bourbon and handed one each to Ed and Louis. It wasn't more than a few seconds before Louis conked out.

Ed raised his glass and said, "Good riddance." He downed his drink and held out the empty glass for a refill.

For the next ten minutes, he recounted the details of finding Farley's truck and meeting Tulie.

"Why'd you wait so long to tell anyone?" Peter asked.

"I haven't exactly been treated with respect around here, ya know."

"I can't believe that you sat on this information. What the hell were you thinking?"

"A decorated NYPD detective knows how to investigate a homicide, but I'm not so sure about these locals. I wanted to do a little checking on my own, first. "

"Did you ever consider your arrogance is the reason you're disrespected?"

"Really, I've solved more homicides in my thirty-three years on the force than you've got hairs on your ass."

No point in arguing with this arrogant bastard. "Why don't we table this for tonight? I'll get in touch with Detective Daniels and we can meet back here in the morning. Ten o'clock okay for you?"

"That works for me."

"See you tomorrow then."

Peter downed another shot before he left a message for Daniels and punched in Stu's phone number. He was about to leave a message when he heard Stu's voice.

"Hold on, hold on, I'm here. Don't hang up."

"It's Peter. Did I reach you at a bad time?"

"Nah, I was in the hot tub. What's up? Have you heard from Louis?"

"Speak of the devil. He's laid out here, snoring away."

"How'd he take the news?"

"He's quiet now, thank God."

"It's that bad, huh?"

"You can't imagine."

"How's the investigation progressing?"

"I'll know more tomorrow. I'm meeting with Daniels and a blowhard retired NYPD Detective who claims he has information that no one else has."

"Let me know how that turns out."

"Will do."

Peter hung up the phone and walked over to the couch. Louis' mouth lolled open and saliva dribbled down the side of his chin. *No telling how long he'll sleep, but I sure don't feel like babysitting.*

He returned to the party room and watched a lively group of revelers on the dance floor, their torsos gyrating to the Macarena. He was tempted to join them, but headed for the *mole pablano* instead.

FORTY-THREE

DETECTIVE DANIELS PLAYED with the creases in his pant legs. "I've got more important things to do than sit here and wait for this Ed Marrone fella."

"I appreciate that you took the time to stop by," Peter said. "Just hang in a few more minutes."

"I came down here as a courtesy to you. Don't like wasting valuable time on a jack-off like Marrone. Still thinks he's riding shotgun in the big city."

Ed burst through the door.

Daniels grunted, "It's about time."

"Sorry I'm late."

Daniels rubbed his hands together. "Let's get this party started. First off, what's this I hear about you withholding evidence? I've got a good mind to take you into custody."

"You've got it all wrong."

"Yeah, just sit down and keep your yap shut."

Daniels glared at Peter. "And I've got a bone to pick with you."

"Me?"

"Why didn't you report a prowler roaming around? You never said one word. Didn't it occur to you there could be a connection to the murder?"

"You have to understand, we've had enough negative publicity. I still have inventory to move," Peter pleaded. "I had no choice but to keep the information in-house."

"Your plan kinda backfired, didn't it?"

"Guess so."

"I promised to keep you up to date." He pointed at Ed. "And when I'm finished talking, you can add whatever the hell you want, to what we probably already know."

Daniels removed a pad from his back pocket, dragged his thumb across his tongue and flipped through several pages. "Details are a bit sketchy, but on the night of the murder the gatehouse security guard *thinks* he recognized Farley in the passenger seat of a dark, compact sedan. Never bothered to ask the driver for his ID. Guard admitted he may have been a little groggy. He often nods off, this being his second job. Past midnight there's not much activity at the gate. Sometime later—again, details are sketchy—he was awakened by the same car leaving the premises. He waived it through and dozed off again."

Peter's face flushed. "I'll get on that as soon as we're through here."

"What about the twenty-four-hour video surveillance at the gate?" Ed asked. "There must be something on the security camera tape?"

Daniels glared at Peter. "Care to address that Mr. Project Manager?"

No response.

"Don't tell me the system's not functioning," Ed said.

"Shit." Peter kicked the wastebasket under his desk. "It's been down for a while. Technical problems."

Daniels frowned. "Great security you have here."

Ed started to get up.

"Sit!" Daniels barked. "I'm not finished." He cleared his throat. "Based on rigor and body temp, and all things considered, time of death is consistent with the reported time frame. What we know for certain is that the murder weapon is a STIHL MS201 C-E chain saw."

Peter winced. "Jesus, how the hell can you be so sure?"

"Photomicroscope used in the autopsy sees all, tells all. Wounds are extensive with a hell of a lot of ragged flesh. Head's attached by a few shreds, but striations, blade pattern and scoring on the bone is consistent with that model. Unfortunately, equipment located on the premises tested negative for blood or tissue. Must have taken the chainsaw with him and disposed of it elsewhere."

Ed waved his hand in an attempt to attract Daniels' attention.

"Put your damn hand down," Daniels said. "I'll tell you when I'm ready for you. Where was I? Oh yeah, a small amount of blood residue was found in one of the maintenance carts, but no distinguishable fingerprints. Murderer must've wrapped the murder weapon in whatever he used to clean the cart with and took everything with him."

Daniels flipped through several more pages before he continued, "Autopsy revealed advanced cirrhosis of the liver. One way or another, Farley was a goner. Toxicology report shows blood alcohol registered .28, nearly three times the legal limit for DUI. Farley would have been severely impaired. It's unlikely he put up a struggle. That's confirmed by the fact that there weren't any defensive wounds on the body."

Peter shrugged. "Why the excessive brutality, why not hit him over the head or stab him?"

"I suspect Farley pissed off this guy real bad. He grabbed whatever weapon was handy, loaded Farley into a service cart, rode out to where we discovered the body and let 'er rip."

"Why go out there to do the deed?"

Ed jumped up from his seat. "The killer probably figured it'd take longer to discover the body and there'd be less chance someone hears the noise. Maybe he was hoping the water would dilute trace evidence."

Daniels rolled his eyes to the ceiling. "Ya think? Hell, give this man a prize."

"I have it from a reliable source," Ed said, "that Farley met this guy at the Sand Dune over on U.S. 441. That's where I found his truck and the witness who can ID the perp—"

Peter interrupted, "Sounds like they drove back here to conclude their business and for whatever reason, the guy went off on Farley."

"You two are real good together," Daniels said. "You oughta team up and get your own reality TV show or better yet, a sitcom."

"We're just trying to help," Ed said, and plopped back down in his chair.

Daniels scowled. "Oh yeah, you're both a big help, all right. You," he pointed at Peter, "you withheld information about the prowler and you," he pointed at Ed, "you failed to report critical evidence in an ongoing homicide investigation."

"I would've stepped up to the plate sooner," Ed said, "wrapped this case up with a big red bow."

"So what stopped you?"

"Sheriff's Office is too pig-headed to consider anything other than the egotistical crap leaking out of their sun-baked brains."

Daniels' scowl gave way to a broad grin. "Sorry to disappoint you, but we've known about Farley's truck and that Tulie gal for awhile now." He stood up and placed the notebook in his back pocket. "Thanks for nothin', boys."

Daniels strode from Peter's office holding his belly. When he could no longer contain himself, he erupted in laughter.

FORTY-FOUR

THE MEETING IN PETER'S OFFICE had been one more reminder that Ed had failed in his attempt to find a post-retirement diversion. After the altercation with Louis and the humiliating face-to-face with Daniels he needed to do some serious thinking.

A half hour on the treadmill seemed like a good idea. He entered the health club through the men's locker room and nodded as he passed several of the men he knew huddled together.

"Don't be in such a hurry," Burt Rosen called out. "Come on over here. I promise you'll thank me."

"What are you guys up to?"

Al Frank smirked. *"Up,* that's the operative word here, right guys?"

The other men nodded.

Ed watched them toast each other with purple pills before they gulped them down.

One of the men called back as he sprinted toward the exit, "Time's a wastin'. I'm outta here."

Another man broke into song, "When I was young and I was hung—"

He was interrupted by a sneaker whizzing past his head.

"What the hell did you guys swallow?" Ed asked.

Bert tossed him a pill. "It's brand new... fewer side effects than the other stuff on the market."

Ed caught the pill on the fly and flipped it back and forth between his thumb and forefinger.

Bert pointed to his crotch. "It's guaranteed to make your pecker hard. Your wife will love it."

The scenario took Ed back to his high school days: young men, their hormones raging, swapping stories of real or imagined conquests along with instructions on how to use a condom. *I can't remember the last time Vicky and I washed each other's backs in the middle of the day. To hell with the treadmill.*

He popped the pill into his mouth and hoped she was in the mood for a little afternoon delight.

FORTY-FIVE

THE DAY HAD BEEN EXHAUSTING, the sun's rays merciless. Hector's flat-brim Marlins cap was as useless as a paper party hat. At the end of his shift his shirt and undershorts stuck to his skin.

He dragged himself across the employee parking lot in the sweltering heat and was about to open his car door when he spotted a piece of paper tucked under the windshield wiper. He retrieved the neatly folded paper before collapsing inside his car. He turned on the ignition and adjusted the A/C control to maximum, leaned his head back, and was about to nod off when he remembered the paper in his hand.

The note read: "Come to my house for supper, *por favor*. 2130 Worth Court. *Muchos comidas y cerveza, frio.*"

Hector peered into the rear-view mirror and raked his fingers through grimy hair. *I look lousy, stink like goat, but is hard to say no to chicken stew and cold beer… and Rosa.* He shifted the car into drive, gunned the engine, and sped out of the parking lot. Gravel pelted the car's undercarriage in time to his racing heart.

* * *

Rosa looked up from stirring seasoning into the aromatic mixture simmering on the stove. She noticed Hector standing outside the screen door and wiped her hands on her apron. She unlatched the door and held it open. "I didn't hear you knock on the front door."

"I dirty from work. Better I come back here."

"I apologize for the short notice," she said. "You'll feel better after you wash up." She led Hector to a small bathroom at the end of the hall.

He picked up a scented bar of soap and inhaled deeply before he lathered his face and arms and vigorously scrubbed away the grime that clung to his skin.

Rosa rapped on the door. "Supper's ready."

Hector dried off using a small cloth towel embroidered with daisies. He hung the damp towel over the side of the sink with the flowers facing out and hurried to the kitchen.

Rosa was already seated at the table. They ate in silence until, with cheeks stuffed full of chicken stew and vegetables, he mumbled, "You cook *muy bien.*"

"You are most welcome. Eat as much as you like."

After dinner, Hector offered to help clear the table.

"Clean-up is faster if I do it myself," Rosa said. "Wait for me in the front room or outside on the porch."

Hector entered the tidy living room. Polished wooden tables, a sofa decorated with crocheted doilies, and a vase filled with fresh flowers made him feel out of place in soiled work clothes.

He stepped onto the dimly lit porch and considered the seating options. He rejected the glider with two cushions and the single rocker, and instead sat down on a porch step. Despite the two beers he'd consumed with supper, his throat felt dry. *What we talk about? Rosa gonna ask me to sit nex' to her on the glider? Then wha' we gonna do?*

He pleaded aloud, *"Madre mia,* my head won' stop talkin'."

Rosa came onto the porch, reached down, and stroked his cheek. "I didn't feed you too much, did I?"

He jumped up. "I mus' go."

"Where you running, little boy... to your *mamacita?*" She placed the palm of her hand over her heart. "Please, wait. I... I feel something for you, here."

Hector's face flushed. *I feel somethin' too, but I no can fin' words.* "Jus' lemme go," he pleaded.

Rosa stood firmly in place and blocked his escape. "Just hear what I have to say," she said. "A woman where I clean... a doctor, she helps people with their problems. I hear her talking with them. Dr. Bennett is caring and smart. She can help you too, I am sure of it."

Hector shook his head. "I go now."

* * *

Hector sat on the edge of his sagging mattress and undressed without turning on the light. Noise filtered in from the turnpike a few yards away. Headlights danced across the translucent window shade hanging haphazardly at the foot of his bed.

He longed for Rosa to comfort him, to rest his cheek against her breast, but he was not worthy of this gentle, caring woman. *She wannna help an' when you with her you estúpido.* He imagined her piercing eyes searching for answers to questions he had often asked himself. *Who are you, Hector Velazquez? What is wrong with you? How long before you prowl through darkness again?*

Many times his mother had told him he was a good person, a loving son. He imagined what she would say if she were here now.

"Is time you grow up, *niño,*" she'd say. "You mus' find your way without me to guide you. True, you are alone, but who is to blame? You have a kind heart, you work hard. Why you don' believe in yourself?"

His sobs came faster and louder until soulful wailing echoed throughout the room.

FORTY-SIX

ROSA COULDN'T STOP thinking about Hector and how poorly the evening at her house had ended. She was beginning to care about him deeply and was certain he had strong feelings for her, as well, which made his abrupt departure even more puzzling.

The next time she cleaned for Dr. Bennett, she asked for a few minutes of her time. Rosa said, "I have a friend…"

Ah, a friend… where have I heard that before? Dr. Bennett thought. "It's not uncommon for clients to reference a 'friend'," she said, "rather than acknowledge they're talking about themselves."

A guileless smile crossed Rosa's lips. "No, no, I do have a friend who needs your help."

"Tell me about this *friend* of yours."

Rosa lowered her gaze. "I'm not sure what is troubling him, but I know it is keeping him from finding joy in his life."

"Has he told you this himself?"

"No, but—"

"Then how can you be certain that he needs help or even wants help?"

"I see it in his eyes."

"It sounds as if you care a great deal for this man."

"In my heart I believe he is a good man."

"Look, Rosa, without more information I can't help your friend or you."

"He is Hector... a maintenance worker."

"Here, at Villa Paraiso?"

"Yes."

"I'd like to help, but—"

"Please, Dr. Bennett, he's touched my heart with a tenderness I've never known. Something draws us together and then..."

Dr. Bennett leaned forward. "And then?"

"He pulls away like... like he's afraid to get close. Please, please, Dr. Bennett, I know you can help him."

Dr. Bennett sighed and opened her appointment book. "Let's see... what time does your friend start work?"

"7:00 a.m."

"And he'll agree to meet with me?"

"I'll make sure that he's here."

"Hmm, let's see... two weeks from today, Thursday looks good. I can see him for a half-hour or so before my first appointment. Tell him to be here at six."

"Thank you so much... but... there is one thing you must know."

"Oh."

"My friend does not have much money."

Dr. Bennett waived her hand. "Don't worry about my fee. The important thing is for Hector to keep his appointment."

"Thank you. Thank you so much. Today, for you, I clean very hard."

"You're welcome. And Rosa..."

"Yes?"

"You always clean very hard."

Rosa hurried toward the laundry room in response to the buzzer that signaled the end of the drying cycle. She folded the warm towels and stacked them in the empty laundry basket, all the while agonizing over how Hector might react after she tells him about his upcoming appointment with Dr. Bennett.

FORTY-SEVEN

AT AGE FIFTY-SEVEN, Dr. Allison Bennett was finally free to make her own life decisions. Her generous divorce settlement allowed her to do whatever she damn well pleased. Working two days a week provided the right amount of mental stimulation she needed to balance her new life of leisure.

On occasion, she'd accepted a new client *pro bono,* something her husband Carl would have never approved of during their marriage. She had once hinted that she planned to treat a friend's nephew who couldn't afford to pay for therapy. Carl had gotten all bent out of shape.

"Are you *both* nuts?" he'd said.

"Please don't use that word," she'd answered. "I'm not nuts and neither is he. It's just that—"

He'd put up his hand. "I'm not interested. And here's another word you won't like, crazy. Are you crazy, working for free?"

"But, Carl—"

"The subject's closed."

* * *

Before she and Carl had met in Graduate school, Allison had believed that love at first sight was a sentimental delusion she attributed to immaturity. That was before she experienced the emotion first-hand.

Sigmund Freud may have argued that she had succumbed to one of humanity's primal instincts: lust.

Carl satisfied her insatiable sexual hunger with endless hours of passionate lovemaking. He surprised her with spontaneous interludes in darkened stairwells, between the campus library's book stacks, and in her dorm room. He snuck through her open window and ravaged her as she slept, or so he thought.

Allison had often feigned slumber and stifled waves of unabated ecstasy until she was satiated. Without warning she'd flip over, mount Carl, and pin his arms above his head for round two. The passion in her marriage had once raged like a blazing inferno, but over time the embers cooled until all that remained were ashes.

It wasn't until she retrieved a pair of Carl's soiled briefs from the bathroom floor that she became aware that someone else had become the recipient of his lust. She plucked the tightly curled, carrot-colored hair protruding from the soft fabric and held the irrefutable evidence up to the light. It in no way resembled her stick-straight, chestnut brown tresses.

Carl had been too busy to notice Allison enter the den. He continued to pound his laptop keys.

"Carl, stop. There's something I need to discuss with you."

"Can't it wait?" he asked without looking up.

"No."

Surprised to hear her raise her voice, he clicked "save" and gave Allison his full attention. "What's so important that you have to interrupt me while I'm working?"

Allison hesitated, knowing full well that a confrontation would surely seal their fate.

Carl glanced at the clock on his desk. "Allison, I don't have time for games."

"I have something to show you."

He slammed the lid on his laptop closed. "What? What, Allison?"

Her hand trembled as she placed the hair on top of his laptop. "Whose hair is this?"

"How the hell should I know?" He made a sweeping gesture with his hand.

Allison grabbed his wrist. She watched as the hair floated to the floor.

They both lunged after it, but she was quicker.

She offered her out-stretched hand. "This… this is what I wanted to show you."

Carl turned his head away and stormed past her. "That's it Allison. I've had all I can take."

After their divorce, and no longer encumbered by the dead horse she had beaten for way too long, Allison transitioned through Kübler-Ross' Five Stages of Grief in record time.

FORTY-EIGHT

HECTOR WORRIED ABOUT the weird noise his car made whenever the engine idled. Manny had promised to stop by after work and check it out. The odometer on the second-hand 1985 Chevy Malibu registered well over 100,000 miles.

Manny stuck his head under the hood and tinkered around for several minutes before he stood up and announced, *"Muy* gunk, *muy* rust. Your car is gonna croak." His eyes rolled back in his head.

"Don' be jokin' with me, man," Hector said.

"Who's jokin'?"

"Ai yai yai, what I gonna do?"

"Mi amigo, I think you buy a bicycle and prepare for the funeral."

Hector shrugged. "Wha' you talkin' 'bout, funeral?"

Manny laughed so hard, tears rolled down his cheeks. "The funeral for when you bury this piece-a-crap."

"Always makin' fun."

"You're too serious. Lighten up. You think my life is any different than yours?"

Hector was grateful for Manny's friendship and thought it best not to answer. Instead, he walked inside the house and grabbed a couple of beers from his assigned shelf in the fridge he shared with the other renters.

He found Manny leaning against the car wiping his hands on a rag. Hector handed him an ice-cold Corona, lifted his own bottle, and drank deeply.

Hector shrugged. "No money for bicycle, so wha' I gonna do?"

"You drive this heap until the end and then you call your *amigo* here and we figure it out together."

The two men clinked bottles.

"You good friend. I no wanna make trouble, but I got 'nother problem."

"What's that?"

"Me, *muy estúpido* when I go Rosa house."

"I help you with your car, now I help you with your Rosa. Tell her you are sorry you act like a donkey's behind."

Hector scratched his head. "Jus' like that?"

"Just like that."

"I happy to know you, my smart friend."

"I am happy to know you too."

The two men clinked bottles again and watched as the last light of day slipped away.

FORTY-NINE

HECTOR HAD STOPPED by Rosa's house unexpectedly and announced, "I mus' talk to you 'bout somethin'."

Rosa sat on the porch glider and waited for him to settle down, but he continued to pace back-and-forth.

"Hector," she said, "I know you're nervous, but tell me what's on your mind and be done with it."

"I 'fraid you laugh."

"Right now, I can use a good laugh," she said. "I think you can too, but I would never laugh at you." She patted the seat next to her.

Hector stopped pacing and sat down. "I tell you. Las' time we together I... I..." He lowered his voice. "I sorry I ac' like donkey's behind."

Rosa burst out laughing.

"You laughin' at me!"

"No, Hector, I'm laughing because I'm happy you're here. I'll accept your apology on one condition."

"Whas that?"

"I made an appointment for you to talk to Dr. Bennett, the smart lady I clean for. You have to promise that you will keep the appointment."

Hector jumped up. "Why you do that, go behin' my back, gossip to stranger?"

"I can no longer be silent. There is something tormenting you."

"Lady, you crazy, *loco in la cabeza.*"

Hector's words stung.

"I only wanted to help you."

"I don' need no help."

"But Hector, you don't see what I see." She reached out to touch him, but he pulled back. "See, this is what I mean. You make believe nothing's wrong, but I know in here..." She beat on her chest, "in here you are hurting."

"Why you care 'bout Hector?"

"The heart knows when a good man needs a helping hand. My heart tells me you're such a man."

Hector swallowed hard.

"You will go Thursday? I promise you won't be sorry. You will go, yes?"

Hector nodded. *For Rosa I go, only for Rosa.*

FIFTY

DURING A RECENT phone conversation, Daniels updated Peter on the murder investigation's progress. "Aside from identifying the type of weapon," he said, "the physical evidence collected at the scene wasn't worth a damn. All we have to go on is information obtained from Sand Dune's bartender. On the night of the murder he recalls seeing a man with Farley. They seemed pretty chummy. Unfortunately, the bartender's description of this guy fit three-quarters of the undocumented workers in South Florida. A large amount of cash in small denominations was found inside the air-conditioning sleeve in Farley's apartment, along with an unloaded revolver registered to him. There was no indication of anything illegal."

Peter had suspected Farley was involved in some sort of questionable activity, but as long as he did his job and no one complained, he'd turned a blind eye and a deaf ear. He had enough on his plate as it was.

Responsibility for running Villa Paraiso rested squarely on his shoulders. More often than not, Louis and Stu were off doing their own thing. Stu had recently completed a leisurely cruise through the Caribbean aboard his fifty-five-foot Sea Ray, accompanied by a stunning model he met at a boat show. Louis occupied his time dropping obscene amounts of money at casinos throughout the country, all the while battling his personal demons. Peter had to keep reminding himself that his current situation wasn't all that bad. Growing up, he had never imagined that one day this scrappy kid from Brooklyn would trade gated storefronts and graffiti tags for an upscale community in Boca Raton.

Each glorious morning, he drove past the ornamental wrought-iron gates where a visual feast awaited—perfectly manicured lawns, gracefully swaying palm trees, exotic flowering plants, and Amy. For the first time in his life, he'd experienced contentment.

FIFTY-ONE

HECTOR'S LIFE IN PURGATORY weighed heavily on his mind. Villa Paraiso had offered endless opportunities to indulge his urges: urges that were becoming increasingly difficult to control. He considered the possibility that Rosa was right about his needing help. He had no choice but to keep his promise to see Dr. Bennett.

The night before his appointment, he had thrashed about in bed for hours. Finally, mentally and physically exhausted, he fell into a fitful sleep only to awaken a short time later.

* * *

At exactly 6 a.m., Hector arrived at Dr. Bennett's villa. He grasped the iron door knocker, took a deep breath and rapped on the door.

The door swung open. "Good morning, Hector. Please come in."

He pulled off his cap and bowed slightly.

The slender woman, dressed in a navy-blue skirt and white sleeveless blouse, led him down a long corridor. She stopped inside an archway leading to a windowless alcove not much bigger than Hector's sleeping room. The walls were lined with bookshelves and official-looking framed documents.

With the sweep of her arm, Dr. Bennett directed Hector to one of two small leather chairs with low curved backs. She sat down in the chair behind her desk.

Hector's breath came in short bursts.

"Please, make yourself comfortable," Dr. Bennett said. She lifted a yellow pad and a pencil from her desk. "Let's begin, shall we? What brings you here today?"

Hector answered in a barely audible voice, "I no sure."

"It's not unusual to feel nervous about what to expect the first time you enter a therapist's office. Gaining your trust is important to me. Confidentiality is equally important. I promise, whatever we discuss here is just between the two of us."

"You won' tell Rosa nothin'?"

"No, Hector. My office is as sacred as the confessional."

Hector had been sitting on the edge of his seat. He slid back and was surprised to find the chair more comfortable than it had appeared.

"What Rosa tell you 'bout me?"

"She didn't say much, just that she's worried about a friend who seems troubled."

Hector sighed.

"You're worried about what Rosa told me?"

"I s'pose," he said.

"Anything else?"

"I 'fraid to come… talk to stranger."

"Now that you're here, have you changed your mind?"

Hector shrugged. "A little."

"Good, I'm glad to hear that. Now tell me what brings you here today?"

Why I here? For me? For Rosa? Hector averted Dr. Bennett's gaze. "I come maybe for sadness, maybe for…"

Dr. Bennett sat with her hands folded in her lap and waited for him to continue.

"I come…" He hesitated, his face stoic.

"Go on Hector. Remember, you're safe here."

No response.

She allowed him a few minutes to gather his thoughts. "Please continue."

Hector's lips trembled, and in a faltering voice he declared, "I… am the one… the one they call… *prowler.*"

Dr. Bennett was caught off guard. "I see," she said, struggling to keep her emotions in check.

Hector shifted in his seat. "I don' feel so good."

"Would you like to rest for a few minutes?"

"No res', I go now."

"All right then, next Thursday we'll begin where we left off."

"*Sí, sí,* nex' time."

Hector quickly retraced his steps to the front door. He fumbled with the door knob and raced down the walkway.

* * *

Dr. Bennett considered that often, clients carried a lifetime of emotional baggage and more than a few dragged a three-piece set. It wasn't unusual for the issue they presented with to be merely a glimpse of underlying turmoil.

She didn't expect Hector to be forthcoming during a first meeting, but then she remembered Rosa's words, "My friend is troubled."

Troubled indeed. What dark secrets have yet to be revealed?

FIFTY-TWO

HECTOR HAD JUST CLOCKED OUT and returned his time card to the rack when Manny waived him over to the podium and held up a pile of paperwork. "Farley's haunting me from the grave," Manny said.

"Wha' you mean?" Hector said.

"I have *my* work and I have to complete reports and file work orders *he* let pile up. Maggie doesn't understand I'm busy with work stuff. She thinks I'm seein' somebody else."

"You still like her, *sí?*"

"Sure." Manny closed his eyes and smacked his lips. "Even if I didn't I'd be crazy to give up free eats."

Instead of driving home for a sparse meal of leftover lentil soup and stale bread, Hector headed to Café Cantina with the intention of smoothing things over between Maggie and Manny. The possibility that he might see Rosa spurred him on. On the way, he rehearsed what he planned to say to Maggie after he arrived. *You wrong 'bout Manny,* he'd say. *He wanna be with you, but he workin' hard.*

Lost in thought, he didn't notice Rosa's car pulling out as he entered the parking lot. He almost clipped her front fender.

Rosa leaned on the horn.

"Loca!" he yelled, loud enough for her to hear.

Rosa lowered her window. "Who you calling crazy?"

"¡Ay! Is you," he said. "Where you goin'?"

"I stopped by for a minute on my way home. Are you hungry?"

Hector nodded.

"Follow me." Rosa shot out of the parking lot.

Explaining to Maggie about Manny would have to wait. Hector made a quick U-turn. The driver behind him blasted his horn and pulled up alongside of Hector's car. Happy to be on his way to Rosa's house, Hector grinned at the man's obscene hand gesture and sped off.

* * *

Rosa set out utensils and gleaming white plates on scalloped place mats. She prepared a cheese omelet with onions and peppers large enough for both of them to share. She slathered sweet butter on crusty chunks of day old bread.

"Have you talked to Dr. Bennett?" she asked.

Hector ran his finger around the rim of his plate. "Uh-huh."

"You like her? You think she can help you?"

"Uh-huh."

"That's it, *uh-huh…* that's all you have to say?"

"No." He pointed to the delicate glass dish filled with guava jelly. "Jelly, *por favor.*"

After dinner, Hector cleared the table and Rosa washed the dishes. She took the last dish from him and grazed his hand with her damp fingertips. She was seized by an unexpected fervor.

She wiped her hands and led Hector toward her bedroom. She flicked a wall switch and the overhead fan hummed in the darkness. They sat down on the bed. She nestled his head against her bosom and whispered, *"Mi amor,* my wish is to be with you forever." She leaned across and turned on a small bedside lamp. "I want to see behind your eyes. I need to know the real Hector."

Locked in a passionate embrace, Rosa guided her tongue as if it were the key to unlock his emotions.

Hector kneaded her supple hips and whimpered. The stirring between his legs became more urgent. He responded like a man who had lived a life without food or drink and happened upon a feast.

They made love long into the night until they drifted off to sleep wrapped in each other's arms.

FIFTY-THREE

THE PREDAWN PROWLER SIGHTINGS continued and the murder investigation appeared to be at a standstill. During a conference call, Peter, Stu, and Louis expressed their concerns. After much debate, they agreed to offer a reward for information leading to the arrest and conviction of Farley's murderer.

"Amy!" Peter called from his office. "Come in here."

Amy missed their playful banter and the occasional pat on her ass, but most of all she missed their lovemaking which had recently hit a slump. She ended her phone conversation and entered Peter's office. One look at his face and it was obvious he was stressed to the max.

"What's up, boss?"

"I need you here." Peter pointed to the side of his desk for emphasis.

She took several exaggerated giant steps and ended up at Peter's side. "I'm here."

"No, you're not. I can tell when your mind's somewhere else."

"You're right. I'm having a problem with the damn copier. Work's backed up. Serviceman just called to say he's on his way over. But if anyone's a million miles away, it's you. You've been distracted and irritable for some time now."

He took her hand in his and tenderly kissed each finger. "I know, I know, I've been acting like an asshole."

"Well… I wouldn't go so far as to say that."

"I've got too much on my mind right now. Between the murder and the prowler, sales have tanked. And on top of everything else, my mother's breaking my chops about coming down for a visit. My place is all the way east which means I'll have to shuttle her all over the place and what is she going to do all day while I'm at work?"

"I've got the perfect solution."

"She can stay at your place?"

"No. Your mom can stay here in one of the furnished models. She can take her meals at the clubhouse and use the facilities. You can see her whenever you have time."

"Not bad, kiddo. Not bad at all." He pulled Amy close, lifted her blouse a few inches and kissed her soft belly. "Sorry, I know I've neglected you."

She kissed the top of his head. "Fix-it guy's coming. Is there anything else before I go?"

"Louis, Stu and I agree," Peter said, "if we offer a reward, someone is bound to step forward with information that will move the investigation along. What do you think?"

"It's certainly worth a try. How much did you have in mind?"

"Ten-thousand smackers."

"Sounds good to me. I think I'll dust off my Sherlock Holmes hat and join in the manhunt."

Peter let out a hearty laugh before he swatted her on the backside. "That's enough chit-chat. Now get back to work."

Amy tucked her blouse into her waistband, feeling confident she and Peter were back on track.

FIFTY-FOUR

HECTOR RECALLED the passion-filled night with Rosa and thrust his naked body onto his thin mattress. He rocked back-and-forth with a sense of urgency. The bed's metal frame groaned. He bit down on the corner of his pillow to stifle sounds of ecstasy for fear God would hear and punish him for *all* of his sins.

The following morning, on the way to Dr. Bennett's office, Hector agonized over what might take place during his visit. *If I lucky, she no remember wha' I say las' week.*

He felt relieved when she didn't bring up his confession, but it didn't take long before relief turned to an overwhelming sense of dread.

"How was your week, Hector?"

"Why you askin'?"

"It's just a question, like 'how are you' or 'how've you been,' but it seems to have deeper meaning for you."

His face flushed. "Good week, I work hard, have a few beers, ya know."

"I *don't* know. That's why I'm asking."

"Oh."

"Did you do anything fun? See a movie, visit a friend?"

He stared at the floor. *"Sí,* a friend, I see a friend."

"Go on."

"Rosa, I see Rosa."

"Did you do anything fun with Rosa?"

Aye. She know I been with Rosa. "Why you askin'?"

"If you don't feel comfortable talking about Rosa, we can talk about something else."

Somethin' else? Madre mia, she no forget the prowler.

Dr. Bennett leaned in closer and cocked her head.

Hector shrugged. "Wha' you wan' me to say?"

"You don't have to say anything unless you want to."

Estúpido! I can no take back my words. Wha' I say now?

"Is Rosa a *special* friend, like a girlfriend?"

Silence.

"Are you *work* friends?"

Hector whispered, "We make love."

"So it sounds as if Rosa is a special friend."

"Sí, muy especial," Hector said. "She show me kindness."

"Kindness is important to you."

"Kindness make me feel good."

"Is Rosa the only person who makes you feel this way?"

He bit his lower lip. "Long, long, ago… when I was boy."

"Remembering makes you sad."

Hector lowered his voice, *"Sí."*

"Tell me about when you were a boy."

His throat tightened. "No now…"

"Would you prefer to talk about something else?"

"Nothin' else. Don' feel so good."

"Are you ill?"

"No sick… jus' feelin' weak."

"Talking about your feelings makes you uncomfortable."

"I go now… no worry."

"Won't you stay awhile longer?"

Hector stood up and hurried out of the room. Before he

opened the front door, he called out, "Nex' Thursday, you will see me?"

"Yes, Hector. I look forward to seeing you again."

Dr. Bennett heard the door slam shut. She tapped her pencil on the yellow pad before she noted: *client's not always engaged or participatory. Clearly, traditional talk therapy intensifies his resistance. Next session hypnotherapy.*

Her intuition told her that Hector's essence, his true character, lay just below the surface. She was anxious to peel back the layers.

FIFTY-FIVE

THE INTRICATE ICE SCULPTURE displayed in La Piazza's entranceway heralded a bountiful feast, sure to please every palette. Villa Paraiso's legendary Sunday brunch offered a spectacular array of culinary delights.

Ed and Vicky had invited Al Frank to join them. Al pointed toward the entrance. "Hey, I just saw Rick walk in. Is it okay if I ask him to join us?"

"Sure, wave him over," Ed said. "I haven't seen him in a while. Wonder what he's been up to?"

Before Al had had a chance to attract Rick's attention, a willowy brunette wearing a cream-colored dress decorated with iridescent sequins draped her arm around Rick's neck. The considerably younger woman in the skin-tight dress, which left little to the imagination, caressed Rick's face and kissed him full on the lips.

Al gawked. "Guess that answers your question."

Ed nodded. "That's for damn sure."

"In case you haven't noticed," Vicky said, "she's a little overdressed for Sunday brunch."

Ed winked at Al. "Could be Rick invited her for a sleepover and she didn't have a thing to wear... no PJ's, no nothin'."

Vicky playfully poked Ed's arm. "I'll leave you two boys to your fantasies."

She flitted between serving stations trying to decide where to begin her gastronomical adventure. Her eyes grew wide when she spotted someone carrying her favorite childhood treat, a waffle slathered with peanut butter and topped with sliced banana. She grabbed an empty plate and waited impatiently for the three people on line ahead of her to place their order at the omelet station.

Vicky recalled a time when she had been a skinny, listless, kid. Her pediatrician had prescribed a tonic to increase her appetite. *He should see me now,* she thought. *He'd pee his pants.*

She carried her treasure back to the table. "I'll have to starve myself for two days after I eat this, but it's worth it."

"You think maybe you should add another day?" Ed teased.

Vicky glared at him. "That's cold, Ed."

"See, Al," Ed said, "this is what happens after you're married for awhile." Ed tugged at an imaginary necktie. "No respect, I don't get no respect."

Al laughed at Ed's pitiful impression of Rodney Dangerfield. "I think I'd like to give marriage a try someday."

"Take my wife, please," Ed said, imitating another deceased funnyman.

They ate with gusto, stopping only long enough to glimpse plates piled high with mouth-watering entrees and spectacular desserts carried past their table.

"Say, Al, don't you have those two sisters living across the street from you?"

"Yeah, I've been meaning to introduce myself."

Vicky tilted her head in the direction of Rick's table. "I bet Ricky Ricardo over there would've bedded them both by now. We should have a get-together at our house with pigs-in-a-blanket and cocktails. Who knows, maybe before the end of the night there could be a few pigs *under* the blanket."

"Better ease up on the mimosas, babe," Ed said.

Vicky ignored Ed and waived her empty glass to get the server's attention.

"Sorry, Al, she's always been outspoken, but since I started poppin' those little purple pills, she's turned into a wild woman."

Al gave Ed a knowing look. He was beginning to feel a little wild himself. He imagined a cocktail party where he and the newly arrived sisters engaged in a ménage à trois smack in the middle of Ed and Vicky's living room.

FIFTY-SIX

DR. BENNETT USHERED HECTOR into her office, but instead of sitting at her desk, she took the seat opposite him in one of the small leather chairs.

"Today," she said, "I'm going to help you relax and focus inward. Instead of talking about things you experience in the present, we'll revisit events from your past."

Hector wasn't sure he understood what Dr. Bennett meant, but he remembered the promise she had made the day they met. *You are safe here.* He was prepared to do whatever it took to keep Rosa in his life.

Dr. Bennett spoke slowly and softly, "The only thing you hear is the sound of my voice. Your feet are flat on the floor. Take a deep breath through your nose. Feel the air circle around in your lungs. Slowly breathe out through your mouth."

Hector did as he was told.

"Your eyes are growing tired… your eyelids heavy. Your arm muscles are beginning to relax… now your leg muscles. Feel the tension leave your body."

Hector imagined his chair caressing his lower back. His clenched fingers unfolded.

"The sensations you feel are pleasurable," she went on. "Feel the warmth of the sun on your face."

Hector tilted his head back.

"How does that make you feel?"

"Muy bueno."

"Yes, Hector... peace and comfort bring you satisfaction. You're near a body of water. Hear the waves break against the shoreline. Let the water flow over your toes. Can you feel the sand ripple beneath your feet?"

He shuffled his feet.

Dr. Bennett leaned forward. "Where is this place?"

Hector sighed.

"Hector, can you tell me where you are?"

Tears streamed down his cheeks.

Dr. Bennett lowered her voice. "This place where you're standing, where is it?"

Hector shuddered.

"It's okay Hector, you're safe. You can tell me where you are."

He took a deep breath. "I home."

Now we're getting somewhere, Dr. Bennett thought, uncertain if she should continue or wait until next week before delving deeper. She spoke slowly and softly, "The only thing you hear is the sound of my voice. Feel the warmth of the sun. Feel your arms and legs relax. On the count of three your eyelids will no longer feel heavy. You will awake feeling refreshed, one... two... three."

Hector rubbed his eyes like a child awakened from a nap. He appeared bewildered as he ran his hands along the sides of his cheeks and felt dampness.

"How do you feel, Hector?"

"I... I feel okay."

"Good."

"Dr. Bennett..."

"Yes, Hector?"

"Was I sleepin'?"

"You were… relaxing."

"Glad I wasn' sleepin'"

"Why is that?"

Hector chuckled, "You workin', Dr. Bennett. No nice if I sleepin' and you workin'."

Dr. Bennett smiled. *Aha! The man has a sense of humor.* "I'd like to end a little early today. I'll see you next Thursday at six."

"*Sí,*" Hector said and stood to leave. "Thursday at six."

FIFTY-SEVEN

ROSA WIELDED A CAN of ant and roach spray with one hand and worked a wet mop laced with disinfectant across The Equator's concrete floor with the other. From time to time she stopped and shook her head. The scarred surface didn't appear any cleaner than before she'd washed it. The bathrooms weren't much better. She compared them to the bathrooms in the clubhouse. Money, education, and ethnicity apparently had no bearing on bathroom etiquette. The only difference was that women peed on the seat and men peed all over the floor.

A huge Palmetto bug scurried across her mop and disappeared into a storage area. Rosa gave chase. She closed one eye and aimed the spray-can with deadly accuracy. The dazed insect hesitated long enough for her to stomp on its hard shell. *Crunch!* She ground in her heel for good measure, then scooped up the residue with a tissue and placed the unexpected treat in the trash can for the ant army marching up and down the receptacle.

Rosa bumped into an open carton protruding from a lower shelf. The carton toppled over and some of the contents spilled onto the floor. She eyed a small, spiral-bound notebook before picking it up, righting the carton, and replacing the spilled bags. *Why would anyone put this in with trash bags unless they were hiding it?*

She hoisted herself up onto Farley's stool, opened the notebook and placed it on the podium. She slowly turned the pages headed in red ink:

NAME, DATE, AMOUNT, INTEREST, PAID, BALANCE

There was no question she'd found a record of loans and repayments that could prove helpful in the murder investigation.

"So," she said to herself, *"that's* what Farley was into. He not only took kickbacks, he was a loan shark. Maybe that's what got him killed."

"Who you talkin' to?"

The sound of Manny's voice startled Rosa. She slipped the notebook into her pocket and hopped off the stool. "Manny, I didn't hear you come in."

"What are you doin' sittin' on Farley's—I mean *my*—stool?"

"Oh, just resting. I've been trying to clean up, but it's a waste of time. Your guys are a bunch of slobs."

Manny reached for a clipboard and pretended to read a work order. "Rosa, somethin' you wanna say?"

"Like what?"

"You tell me."

Rosa grinned. "You're the best boss ever."

"That's not what I mean." He raised an eyebrow. "What you got there in your pocket?"

"Not now," she said. "Come to the café later tonight."

FIFTY-EIGHT

HECTOR, MANNY, AND ROSA huddled around a table and waited for Maggie to finish setting up for the following day's breakfast rush. Despite the "closed" sign hanging on Café Cantina's front door, they spoke in hushed tones.

"The reward is ten-thousand dollars," Rosa said, "but only if the notebook I found leads to an arrest."

Maggie closed her eyes. "We'll pray that it does."

"I gonna take vacation like *gringo* on TV," Hector said, holding the ketchup bottle up to his mouth. "Now that you famous, whatcha gonna do?" He lowered his voice to a baritone. "Go to Disney World!"

"Be serious," Rosa said. She turned to Manny. "What do *you* think I should do with the notebook?"

"Manny thinks the three of you should claim the reward together," Maggie said. "And don't forget to mention Café Cantina when you're on the five o'clock news."

"I can speak for myself," Manny said.

"So speak," Maggie said. "Who's stopping you?"

"Rosa's legal and she found the notebook," Manny said. "She should be the one to turn it in. Then, out of the goodness of her heart and because I love her sister, she will take us to Disney World."

Maggie swatted Manny on the back of his head.

"Ouch," he said. "Why you doin' that?"

"You never say, 'I love you' before, but now for money you love me?" Maggie retreated to the kitchen.

Manny followed.

Rosa and Hector sat silently and listened to the heated conversation coming from the next room.

It wasn't long before the loud voices subsided and the couple returned to the table holding hands. Manny grinned like a schoolboy after his first kiss.

"Have you two made a decision?" Maggie asked.

Hector shook his head. "I tell Rosa, you do what is best, I done nothin' for the money."

Rosa shrugged. "No matter, the important thing is to help friends. She reached over and touched Hector's arm. "We can fix that old car of yours with the money."

He grinned. "Wha' happen to Disney World?"

Rosa wagged her finger. "Not to worry. I'll take all of us." She glanced at the wall clock. "It's late. Tomorrow's work." She pulled him to his feet. "We have much to talk about."

Outside the café, Rosa gave Hector a kiss filled with promise.

His arms encircled her as he returned the kiss. He hoped their *talk* would continue long into the night.

FIFTY-NINE

HECTOR WAS RUNNING LATE for his Thursday morning appointment with Dr. Bennett. He turned the key in his car's ignition and heard *click-click*.

"Damn junk," he said. "If you no dead, I kill you myself." He exited the car and groped for the hood latch. A piece of rusty hinge broke off in his hand. "Shit man, no today." He tossed the metal scrap into the bushes and lifted the hood.

He tugged at the hoses and belts, pounded the battery contacts with his fist, and slammed down the hood. Back in the car he turned the key in the ignition and pumped the accelerator.

Nada.

He tried again and the engine turned over. He kissed the palm of his hand and patted the dashboard. "I no mean wha' I say. I no kill you. I love you, honey."

* * *

Dr. Bennett wondered if Hector would return for his scheduled appointment, and was pleased to find him standing at her front door promptly at 6 a.m.

They walked down the hallway without speaking and

settled into the small leather chairs. Dr. Bennett noticed Hector's pained expression. "Is there something on your mind you'd like to share?" she asked.

"I worry," he said. "I worry you mad at me 'cause I no say wha' you wan' me to say."

"First," she said, "I'd never be mad at you and second, you're not here to please me. I understand that it's not easy to talk about emotions buried deep inside."

Hector cocked his head. "Deep inside… like stuff in my *abuela's* trunk?"

"Yes, Hector, very much like that. Do you know what your grandmother kept in her trunk?"

Hector licked his bottom lip. "Could be is stuff from long ago. She open trunk and cry."

"Yes, sometimes memories make us sad."

Hector nodded.

"Today I'm going to ask you to use your five senses to paint a picture. You will see, hear, taste, smell, and feel things that remind you of the past. Remember, you're safe here. Whatever we talk about is between the two of us, no one else, understand?"

"Sí, sí, comprendo."

"Now, close your eyes and listen to the sound of my voice. Slowly breathe in and out. Your eyelids are relaxed. Your facial muscles are relaxed. The muscles in your neck, chest, and stomach are relaxed." Dr. Bennett waited until Hector's eyelids stopped twitching. "The muscles in your arms and legs are beginning to relax. You are going into a deep… natural… relaxed state."

Hector's body felt weightless, as if balloons held him aloft.

"Think back to that place where the sun and the sand are warm, where the surf flows gently over your toes, to the place you call 'home'."

Hector's eyelids fluttered.

"Do you see someone?"

"I see…"

"Who do you see?"

"Mi mamacita."

"What is your mother doing?"

"She wave to me."

"Are you coming home from school?"

"No, I play outside. Is suppertime."

"What else do you see?"

"Flour on her hands. She bake sweet rolls for supper."

"Can you smell the rolls?"

Hector sniffs the air and smiles. "Smell honey. *Muy bueno.* Wanna taste."

"What does your mother do after she waves?"

Hector's face twisted into a grotesque mask. "Wipe her hands on her apron, try to kiss my cheek," he said. "I pull away. We laugh. I go in house."

"Is anyone else there?"

"No, jus' me an' *mi mama.*"

"Do you hear something?"

No response.

"Tell me what you hear."

"The truck… I hear *mi papas's* truck."

"Your father's home for supper?"

Hector's breathing became labored. He pushed back in his chair. "Rolls… the supper… no ready."

"Take your time," Dr. Bennett said, "breathe slowly."

Hector shuddered. "I… I 'fraid."

"Are you scared of your father? Afraid of what he'll do to you?"

Hector's body tensed. He clutched the armrests. "No… no 'fraid for me."

"What's happening Hector?"

"*Mi papa spit on mi mama,* hit her with fist. She yell, 'Run! Hide!'" Hector bit his lower lip.

"Go on, Hector."

Hector's heartbeat quickened. "I no wan' leave her. Again, she yell, 'Go!' I run outside, but I no hide."

"What do you do?"

"I look… I look in window. She cover eyes. She scream, '*No más, no más.*' He drunk. Push her down an' fall. I run inside. Help drag *mi papa* to bed."

"And then?"

"Rolls ready. Supper ready. We eat."

"And your father?"

"He sleepin'."

"And you? What about you? What are you feeling?"

Hector beat his chest with his clenched fist.

"Inside I cry."

"What are you thinking?"

"Thinkin'? I boy… can do nothin'… jus' watch through window."

* * *

Dr. Bennett had planned to spend the afternoon lounging beside the pool. She had promised herself she would put Hector out of her mind. No other client had crept under her skin the way he had. She was perplexed by the troubled young man. He was more than a lonely child: much more.

She stuffed a towel, sunscreen, a professional journal, and a sun visor into her oversized, straw pool bag and set it down next to the front door. The rain clouds gathering overhead had gone unnoticed until she heard rolling thunder. She tossed the bag onto the couch and plopped down beside it.

A few minutes later, she jumped up, grabbed a protein

bar from the pantry and entered her office. She leaned back in her desk chair and tore open the wrapper, exposing a heart-healthy blend of dried fruits and nuts. In between bites she thumbed through her client folders until she located Hector's. For the most part, her session notes read like a Psych 101 primer.

The client struggles with guilt for not doing enough to protect his mother when he was a child. The experience profoundly affects his ability to respond to the world at large in a socially acceptable way. Reframe client's personal narrative and encourage him to confront challenges and develop affirmations that will promote self-compassion and self-acceptance.

"Bull," Dr. Bennett said aloud. "Who the hell am I kidding? There's no happily ever after in Hector's future." She finished the last of the snack bar and discarded the wrapper in the waste basket under her desk. Sure, she thought, in a *perfect* world therapy often leads to enlightenment, but it's not a perfect world—never was and never will be.

SIXTY

ROSA'S HEART POUNDED as she knocked on Peter's office door.

No answer. She knocked again.

Amy entered the outer office. "May I help you?"

Rosa spun around. "Oh, I… I'm here to see Mr. Duke, but his door is closed. I can come back another time."

"I'm certain he's not with anyone." Amy stepped around Rosa and opened the door a few inches. "Peter, one of the maintenance workers would like to speak with you."

Rosa touched her pocket. "I have something to show you."

"Come on in," Peter called. "I don't bite."

Amy opened the door all the way and said, "Go on in."

Rosa walked slowly and stopped a few feet from Peter. He motioned to the chair beside his desk. "You have something for me?" he said.

She pulled the notebook from her pocket and placed it on the desk.

Peter's brow furrowed. "What's this?"

"I found it when I was cleaning the maintenance shed. I think it is important."

Peter picked up the notebook and turned several pages.

Neat columns listed employees' names and a record of money borrowed and repaid in installments.

"I suppose it's possible this belonged to Farley," Peter said. "He's the only one around here who used a red pen."

"I'm thinking the same thing," Rosa said. "It is possible the murderer knew he kept cash in his office and killed him for the money."

Peter held up the notebook. "Or else he didn't find any money and became enraged."

"I think another reason is possible."

"What's that?"

Rosa said, "I see Eduardo owed much money, more than anyone else."

Peter turned a few more pages and, sure enough, Eduardo appeared to be Farley's best customer. "Sure seems that way," he said.

"You will see that the Sheriff gets this?" she said.

He answered, "Leave it to me."

"And then I will get the reward?"

"I'll be certain to notify you if that's the case."

Rosa thanked Peter for his time and made a hasty exit.

There was no doubt that she had uncovered crucial evidence, but that didn't stop Peter from toying with the idea of claiming the reward as his own. The first thing he'd do with the money was to buy Amy a special gift. But the more he thought about it, the more he realized if he screwed Rosa out of the reward he'd never be able to face Amy.

* * *

Later that evening, Rosa and Hector sat at her kitchen table drinking coffee and eating sweet rolls.

Rosa shook her head and said, "I hope I did the right thing. I was so nervous talking to Mr. Duke.

Hector balled his hand into a fist. "Did he say somethin', do somethin' to scare you?"

"No, but I was worried he'd accuse me of snooping. I am happy it's over and we can move ahead."

Hector laughed nervously. "What you mean, move ahead? Where we goin'?"

"Don't you think we can be happy together?"

Hector swallowed hard. "We happy now. We laugh, make love..."

"You're right," she said, "but that's not enough. I want more."

Hector's face paled. "*¿Por qué?*"

"What do you mean, *why?* That's what people do when they love each other, they get married. After the other night I was certain—Oh! I'm such a fool."

Hector came around the table and bent down beside Rosa. Rosa kissed his cheek. "Come. We will talk."

She took his hand in hers and led him to her bedroom. Throughout the night snippets of conversation punctuated their tender lovemaking.

SIXTY-ONE

PETER FOUND HIMSELF immersed in a plumbing nightmare on the same day his mother was scheduled to arrive. Sometime during the night, the toilet tank in his private office had malfunctioned. The carpet in the outer office had absorbed most of the excess water, but his office resembled a dank swamp.

He sprinted across the soggy carpet. His Bruno Magli loafers sloshed with each step he took and his sopping wet pants cuffs clung to his ankles. He reached behind the toilet and turned off the water supply.

Amy arrived for work and froze in the doorway, mouth agape. She held up her hand to stop curious office staff from entering.

"Look at this," Peter said, pointing frantically at the devastating scene. He swatted his forehead. "Just look at this mess. And it had to happen on the day my mother's flying in."

"Anything I can I do to help?"

"Keep everyone outside and get maintenance over here, and one more thing."

"What's that?"

"There's no way I can leave to pick up my mother."

"Don't worry. I'll take care of it."

* * *

Peter's mother sounded disappointed when he called to tell her he was dealing with a crisis and Amy would meet her at the terminal when she arrived.

"I don't understand why you can't take a half hour and come yourself. I don't know this Amy person and I don't feel comfortable driving with a stranger."

"Ma, give me a break. I've got an emergency here."

"You can't spare a half hour?"

"Ma, Amy's not a stranger. She's like my right arm."

"Okay, okay, I'll ride with your right arm."

"Ma," he groaned.

"I love you, Pumpkin."

"Love you too, Ma. See you soon."

His mother hadn't called him "Pumpkin" since he was a scrawny kid in elementary school. His classmates teased him about his stick-like arms and legs, but he could count on his mother to comfort him. She'd say, "Aww, Pumpkin, don't let them brats bother you. Someday you'll show 'em all."

Peter was reminded of his current predicament when Manny and another maintenance worker entered his office with a Wet Vac and several electric fans. Manny took charge and Pumpkin let out a deep sigh. Now, he could finally relax and enjoy his mother's visit.

SIXTY-TWO

EVERY SO OFTEN, Roger toyed with the idea of entering into a new business venture. He'd accompany real estate agents who droned on and on about how a particular location was well-suited to his needs when it was obvious they were delusional, full of crap, or both.

Despite the heat and humidity, the attractive young woman standing next to Roger wore a turquoise blazer with the name of the company she represented emblazoned across the breast pocket. She appeared unfazed by the oppressive heat and the passing freight and passenger trains that ran alongside Dixie Highway and interrupted their conversation.

Roger shielded his eyes from the glaring sun. "Let's go," he said. "I've seen enough for one day."

"Mr. Bell," she said, "you can't tell me you don't recognize this property's potential."

"It's not exactly what I had in mind."

"Didn't you say you ran a thriving business back in Boston?"

"Yes, I did."

"Then I'd think you'd have the foresight—"

"Look, miss, I don't mean to be rude, but I find that

neon sign two doors down offensive. Naughty Nellie's Nest? Really?"

"But your tearoom's a daytime operation," she said. "The sign isn't illuminated until sundown."

"Still, this location is unacceptable."

"I'm willing to cut my commission."

"Not interested."

The agent tapped on her iPhone. "Give me a minute. I'm sure I can convince the owner to reduce the price."

Roger knew enough about women to recognize they'd never feel comfortable visiting a tearoom adjacent to a railroad crossing or down the street from a titty bar. He threw up his hands. "That's it. I've seen enough."

After another grueling morning in the company of an aggressive real estate agent, Roger had second thoughts about wasting glorious, sunny days cutting crusts off dainty tea sandwiches. He drove passed a billboard advertising an indoor antique and collectable fair and turned off at the next exit. He paid his admission and entered the exhibition hall where he followed the aroma of freshly baked pastries. His mouth watered, but still full from breakfast, he resisted temptation.

He wandered up and down the aisles, stopping from time-to-time to admire an object de art that caught his attention. A distinguished looking, somewhat older gentleman pointed to the Satsuma incense burner Roger held in his hand. "That's a lovely piece you have there," the man said.

"We share the same taste in Japanese pottery," Roger replied.

"Seems that way, but you saw it first."

"I'm just browsing," Roger said and handed the incense burner to the man.

He turned it slowly. "It's beautiful. In the 1940's it was quite common to find Satsuma in almost every household.

Despite the fact that each piece is painstakingly hand-painted, it was relatively inexpensive and available at five-and-dime stores."

Roger pointed to the price sticker. "Considering Satsuma's humble beginnings, it has appreciated considerably."

The man nodded. "I detect a New England accent. Where you from?"

"Boston. By the way, I'm Roger and you are…"

"Samuel."

Roger's stomach fluttered as he drank in Samuel's flawless complexion and brilliant white, perfectly aligned teeth. Samuel placed the incense burner back on the display shelf and the two men shook hands.

Samuel was the first to let go. "Why don't we grab a coffee and get better acquainted?"

"Good idea."

Samuel threaded his way past shoppers milling around vendor's booths. Roger hurried to keep pace.

Samuel turned to see if Roger had followed and smiled when he saw him trailing close behind.

The snack bar area bustled with mid-day activity. The smell of grilled hamburgers and hot dogs intermingled with freshly brewed coffee and buttery-rich pastries. "This place takes me back to when I was a kid and my parents took me to the county fair," Samuel said. "All that's missing is cotton candy and a prize-winning cow."

Roger sniffed the air. "My mouth is watering for something that I spotted earlier." He pointed to a kiosk off to the side of the snack bar.

"You're right," Samuel said, "that smell is irresistible. I'm usually careful about what I eat, but it doesn't take much for me to fall off the wagon."

They negotiated with their respective consciences and each other, and agreed to share one pastry.

Samuel removed a monogrammed money clip from his pants pocket. "I'll get the pastry. Why don't you grab the coffees and I'll find us a place to sit. I take mine black with one sweetener." He held out a twenty-dollar bill which Roger declined.

Roger hurried toward the "Place Order" sign hanging from the ceiling above the counter. After he paid for the coffees, he found Samuel seated at a high-top table set with paper napkins and plastic utensils. Samuel had divided the pastry into two equal portions.

Roger placed the coffee containers and several packets of sweetener on the table and hoisted himself onto the stool opposite Samuel. Samuel tore open a packet of Splenda and stirred the contents into his Styrofoam cup. "I'm surprised I haven't bumped into you before today."

"This is my first time here."

"I don't mean here. You know… out and about, socially."

How can I explain to this devilishly handsome man that I'm restricted to one night out each week to socialize? "I'm new to the area. I'm still getting acclimated to my surroundings."

"Aha! I guess that explains it."

"Where are you from?"

"Originally, the Florida Panhandle, but when I'm not searching for antiquities to satisfy my embarrassingly wealthy client's discerning tastes, I divide my time between Palm Beach and New Jersey." A sheepish grin appeared on Samuel's face. "I wouldn't mind having a personable young man like you accompany me on business trips to Asia and Europe."

Heat rose along the back of Roger's neck. Samuel's thick head of hair, graying at the temples and inviting brown eyes were a definite turn-on. "Sounds like an interesting proposition." He didn't want their conversation to end: not then, not ever.

Samuel glanced at his watch. He reached into his shirt

pocket and extracted a Montblanc pen and two business cards. He slid them across the table with one card turned face-down. "I have to go, but I'd like to see you again. Please jot down your number on the back. The other card has my contact information."

Roger wrote down his cell number.

Samuel's hand lingered on Roger's before he retrieved the card and pen. "I meant what I said about wanting to see you."

Roger gazed into Samuel's eyes. "The feeling is mutual."

* * *

During Samuel's return trip to South Florida, the two men met for brunch and cozy dinners at out-of-the way places, always ending in trysts at Samuel's hotel suite. Roger looked forward to his future with this wonderful man who fulfilled him in every way, but their relationship wasn't without complications.

Samuel and his wife lived in a restored, 18th century English manor house in Short Hills, New Jersey. He had no intention of disrupting his forty-two-year marriage. He planned to discretely sequester Roger in a studio apartment in lower Manhattan and introduce him to business associates as his assistant. Roger's own immediate concern was his mother's reaction to the exciting changes that were about to take place in his life. Breaking the news would be difficult enough without having to explain he had fallen in love with a man who lives on the down low and denies his bisexuality.

* * *

Roger soon learned that overt signs of affection were a no-no, and awkward moments the norm. It wasn't unusual for Samuel to stop in the middle of their conversation or when they were in bed and retreat to the bathroom to answer a phone call from his wife. Afterwards, he'd apologize and attempt to pick up where they left off.

"I'm truly sorry," Samuel said, and slid his hand under the sheet.

Roger pulled away. "Why can't you let the damn phone go to voice mail?"

"Believe me, I'd like to, but that's not possible. We've discussed this before. If you object to the way things are, we have to end our relationship."

Samuel pulled back the sheet and flicked his tongue along Roger's belly, stopping briefly to blow air into his navel. Roger closed his eyes and arched his back, lost in a world where reason no longer existed and ecstasy rules.

Sharing Samuel with his wife would be a challenge, but relinquishing the love of his life wasn't an option.

SIXTY-THREE

SAMUEL HAD AGREED to attend Key West's annual Fantasy Fest—with one caveat: that neither he nor Roger would wear costumes or participate in the festivities. They would observe the Grand Parade from the starting point on Whitehead Street before it burst onto the mile-long stretch of Duval, and nothing more.

Roger was disappointed when he found out they wouldn't be attending the Royal Coronation Ball where the King and Queen of Fantasy are chosen. He had to remind himself that despite trading his mother's restrictions for Samuel's, half a loaf is better than none.

After they arrived in Key West, Samuel suggested a leisurely stroll over to Hog's Breath Saloon for a snack.

"Did I hear you correctly?" Roger asked. "You're actually breaking protocol and eating in the middle of the afternoon?"

"This is one of those occasions when I allow myself to fall off the wagon," Samuel said. "The Saloon's chili dogs are impossible to resist."

"You've been here before?"

"Not recently."

Roger lowered his eyes. "Were you with someone special?"

Samuel cupped Roger's chin in his hand. "I'm here with you now. That's all that matters."

Roger nodded.

Samuel said, "How about that chili dog, but before we go, please promise you won't let me eat more than one."

Roger raised his right hand. "You have my word."

Outside the hotel, two brilliantly colored roosters chased each other and barely missed running across Roger's open-toe sandals. He jumped back. "What the hell?"

Samuel pointed to a mother hen trotting along the curb followed by several fluffy yellow chicks struggling to keep up. "Here comes the mama. Wonder which one of the roosters is the Baby Daddy." He muffled a laugh.

"It must get annoying."

"What?"

"The chickens," Roger said, "they're all over the place."

"They're wild feral chickens, not good for eating. And speaking of eating, let's get a move-on. And don't be surprised if you hear crowing at any hour of the day or night."

"Can't the locals do anything to get rid of them?"

"No, can't do a damn thing," Samuel said. "Strict cruelty law protects them."

"How much farther do we have to go?"

"We're almost there. Turn at the next corner. I can taste that chili dog already."

* * *

Later that afternoon, Roger and Samuel strolled through Mallory Square, their arms held stiffly at their sides. Roger observed other couples displaying signs of affection, and longed for Samuel's arm around him. He didn't notice the wayward rooster crossing their path until it was too late.

The fowl screeched, franticly flapped its wings and

propelled itself upward, making contact with Roger's shin on the way down. Samuel reached out to stop Roger from stumbling.

"I've never been attacked by roosters before," Roger said, "and twice in one day, no less. It must be my sex appeal."

"I can assure you, it's that and more."

Roger's face flushed.

Samuel grasped Roger's hand. "You do know I love you?"

"I know. I love you too."

They exchanged their first public kiss as the sun, like a huge coin borrowed and then returned to nature's piggybank, dipped behind the horizon.

SIXTY-FOUR

PEGGY BEGAN TO NOTICE subtle changes in Roger's habits. He slept in more and spent longer periods of time away from Villa Paraiso. She had come to rely on his presence, especially at dinnertime. She felt a twinge of jealousy for whomever or whatever was robbing her of her son's companionship.

Roger called from the open doorway, "Going out mom, I'll see you later."

"Roger dear," she said. "I'd like to speak with you."

"I'm in a bit of a rush. We'll talk later, I promise."

"Will I see you for dinner?"

"I'm not sure what time I'll be back."

Peggy forced a smile. "Have fun."

"Why don't you and that woman I heard you mention a couple of times get together for dinner at the clubhouse?"

"You mean Emily?"

"Yeah, I guess. Look ma, I have to go. If I'm back early enough I'll join you."

Peggy heard the garage door rumble and hurried to the picture window in the living room. She watched as Roger pulled out in his low slung, convertible two-seater. It reminded her of when he was four years old. His father had come home with a toy car operated by pumping pedals suspended underneath the chassis. She recalled Roger's excitement and the love that filled their home. Now, standing all alone, she was aware of the brittle silence interrupted by the beat of her lonely heart, and the knowledge that she was losing the one person she had hoped would be a part of her life forever.

* * *

The phone on the other end rang five times. Peggy was about to hang up when she heard Emily's voice say, "Hello, hello, don't hang up."

"Sounds like you've been running," Peggy said.

"Oh, Peggy! It's you. I'm chasing a lizard around the house with a broom, but I'm getting too old for this stuff."

"Aren't we all."

"What's wrong? You sound a bit down in the dumps."

"Not really."

Emily wondered if Peggy's mood had something to do with her son Roger. There had been rumors about the couple's relationship, followed by speculation about Roger's sexual orientation. Emily had never known anyone who admitted to having a gay offspring. She was more than a little curious, but not enough to risk losing a budding friendship by asking intrusive questions. She considered herself to be non-judgmental, but imagined how difficult it must be for the individuals involved.

"I don't mean to pry," Emily said, "but if you need a sympathetic ear I'm a good listener… that is, when I'm not hunting big game."

"I know," Peggy said. "You're a sweetheart. It's been a while since I've seen you and I was wondering if you're free for dinner this evening."

"I'm always up for a dinner invitation. I hate eating alone since Harry passed on. Count me in and would it be all right if I invite someone to join us?"

"Sure, who do you have in mind?"

"I met a lovely woman at a 'Laugh Your Way to Good Health' lecture. We laughed so hard I did the pee-pee dance on my way to the bathroom. Anyhow, Theresa is here visiting her son, Peter Duke."

"Is she a widow?" Peggy asked.

"Unfortunately, yes."

"We gals have to stick together. El Greco's around five-thirty?"

"Sounds good to me," Emily said. "I assume Roger will drop you off at the clubhouse."

"No, but I can use some exercise. The clubhouse isn't far. I can walk."

"Don't be silly. If you need a ride, I'll be happy to pick you up."

"If it isn't too much trouble I'd appreciate a ride home."

"No trouble at all. See you over there."

Peggy let out a huge sigh. *There now, that wasn't so hard to do. I not only have dinner plans, but I'll get in a little exercise to boot.*

She checked the time, settled into her recliner, and held out the TV remote. She clicked on one of her favorite programs, a heart-wrenching reality show in which guests reveal their deepest, darkest secrets. As usual, she dozed off before the first commercial break.

SIXTY-FIVE

PEGGY ARRIVED AT THE CLUBHOUSE a few minutes early. She waited across from El Greco's entrance and fidgeted with her purse strap. Emily and her new friend were nowhere in sight. Standing all alone, Peggy felt vulnerable and more than a little annoyed at Roger.

Several of the residents acknowledged her with a nod or a smile. She imagined she'd soon be the topic of their dinner conversation. *Tsk tsk. That poor woman is all alone.*

She hurried down the hall and entered the women's bathroom. Individual foil packets of scented wipes and hand lotion were arranged on an ornate mirrored tray atop a pedestal table. She chose a lavender wipe, tore open the packet, and patted the moist cloth along her neck. *I can't imagine how other women survive without a man at their side. At least I have Roger... well,* had *Roger.*

The door swung open. "I told you we'd find her in here," Emily called over her shoulder. A moment later, Theresa stepped through the doorway and Emily introduced the two women to each other.

On their way to the dining room, Peggy admired Theresa's colorful outfit and strappy sandals that contrasted dramatically with her own outdated polyester dress and sensible shoes. Emily wore a trendy asymmetrical blouse over her slacks. Peggy made a mental note to clip the sale coupons from Friday's paper and do some serious clothes shopping.

The women didn't have to wait long before the *maître d'* led them to a cozy corner table. No sooner had they sat down when ice water accompanied by a basket of warm corn bread, honey-butter, and currant marmalade was placed in front of them.

"Good evening, ladies," a man said. "I'm Jeff. I'll be your waiter." He handed them each a menu. "Tonight's theme is 'Comfort Food'. I'll be right back to answer any questions and take your orders." He flashed the women a toothy grin before he turned his attention to another table.

"I didn't realize that tonight's a theme night," Peggy said.

Emily put on her reading glasses. "Me neither and I usually don't eat these foods."

"What do *you* think, Theresa?" Peggy asked.

"What do *I* think?" Theresa said. "This menu can use a serious infusion of Sicilian cuisine. A nice lasagna smothered in fresh mozzarella or sausage with peppers and onions… now that's comfort food I can get excited about."

Emily snickered, "Chicken fried steak, gravy and biscuits, who do they think we are, farm hands?"

Peggy massaged her chest. "The fried chicken sounds tempting, but I'll have to remove the best part, the crispy skin."

"The *best* part is the Italian Red I'm ordering for us, perfect with fried chicken and curing *agita*," Theresa said.

Emily wrinkled her nose. "I'm not much of a drinker, maybe a little sweet wine on special occasions."

"Isn't red wine paired with beef?" Peggy asked.

Theresa laughed. "Where I come from, red wine goes with anything and everything."

The waiter returned to the table and flashed another toothy grin. "Are we ready, ladies?"

"We'll have three orders of fried chicken, mac and cheese, and a nice bottle of moderately priced Italian Red," Theresa said in an authoritative voice.

Peggy glanced back at El Greco's entrance, hoping to see Roger.

The waiter retuned to the table and uncorked a bottle of Valpolicella. He poured a small amount into Theresa's wine glass. She held her glass up to the light and swirled the ruby-red contents around-and-around before she put the glass to her lips. *"Magnifico!"*

The waiter bowed slightly and served the wine.

Theresa raised her glass. "To my new friends, *salute."* She downed the contents in three gulps.

I can learn a lot from this formidable woman, Peggy thought. "I admire your confidence," she said. "I wish I could be more like you."

Emily took a tiny sip of wine. "Me too."

"You think this confidence came easy? Uh uh… not on your life. It took years to develop. My husband's been out of the picture for a long time, that bastard. I had no choice but to sink or swim. I went from slinging hash in a truck stop and enduring all kinds of abuse from male customers, to managing one of the largest diners in Brooklyn."

Peggy put her hand to her mouth. "Oh my."

Theresa lowered her voice. "Along the way, every inch of me was patted or pinched. I earned those tips. I put in long hours to support my two kids, but it was worth it."

"Didn't they resent you for not being home?" Emily asked.

"At first, yes, but eventually they got used to the babysitter. She let them eat as many store-bought cookies as they wanted. Before that, mama's home-made treats came with a two-cookie limit. My Peter, Jr. and my Jeanne survived."

"I still envy you," Peggy said. "I doubt that I have what it takes to accomplish what you did."

"With a little practice, you too can become an independent woman."

"I'm not so sure. I don't feel complete without a husband."

"Baloney. That's your excuse for avoiding life."

"You think so?"

"I know so. All you need is a sincere desire to change. Just stick with me, kiddo. Miracles do happen."

The waiter arrived with their dinner served family style. He set down platters of steaming hot food in the center of the table. "Hearty appetite and if you need anything let me know," he said.

Peggy pierced a drumstick with her fork and placed it on her plate. The aroma of rosemary and sage made her mouth water. Each time she tried to cut off a piece the leg rocked this way and that.

"Dear," Theresa said, "it's okay to eat fried chicken with your fingers." She lifted a piece of thigh meat to her mouth.

Peggy took the drumstick between her thumbs and forefingers and bit into it.

Theresa toasted Peggy, saying, "I told you, it doesn't take much to change."

Peggy raised the drumstick in one hand and her wine glass in the other. "Here's to you, Theresa, and to independence."

The women continued to eat and gossip until they agreed they couldn't swallow another bite. Theresa signaled for the table to be cleared.

Jeff arrived with a dessert cart and proceeded to describe each offering as if it were a precious jewel.

Theresa covered her mouth with her hand and stifled a belch. "Sorry. I didn't see that coming."

"I know I shouldn't eat another morsel, but that apple-cranberry pie looks irresistible," Emily said.

Peggy extracted a roll of Tums from her purse and

popped one into her mouth. "It is tempting, but I'm afraid if I eat one more thing I'll be struck by lightning."

"Oh, the hell with it," Theresa said, "the slices look large enough to share."

The waiter leaned in. "One serving of apple-cranberry divided in three?"

The other women were surprised to hear Peggy answer for all of them, "Thank you, Jeff, that's a wonderful idea."

"I don't remember when I've had a more enjoyable evening," Emily said, and lifted her glass. This time she took two sips.

SIXTY-SIX

BEFORE HER VISIT, THERESA had been content to live in the sprawling ranch-style house in suburbia that Peter had purchased for her. She had occupied herself with housekeeping, gardening, playing cards at the senior center, and attending church functions. Her daughter and grandson rarely made the long trek to visit her. Most evenings, she ate alone and afterwards dozed off watching TV.

Shortly after she arrived at Villa Paraiso, Theresa began to question her life back home, especially after her *independent women* declaration at dinner the other evening.

Despite South Florida's reputation for being God's waiting room, what better place was there to wait for the inevitable? She reveled in her new surroundings, the liberating relaxed pace, and absence of grime and graffiti. She especially appreciated not having to bundle up in a puffy, down-filled winter coat that made her appear two sizes larger. She was convinced she looked younger and more vibrant than she had in years. The hourglass figure she'd flaunted during her waitress days was still evident, except some of the sand had settled to the bottom.

After Peter's assistant, Amy, had accompanied her on a shopping spree, her wardrobe boasted bold floral prints and geometric patterns in vibrant shades of lime, cherry, and magenta, embellished with sequins and beads. Matching sandals and purses and clunky necklaces and earrings made her feel like a child playing dress-up in her mother's closet. Only her mother would never have imagined a wardrobe in a profusion of colors that rivaled a rainbow's.

* * *

Theresa threw open the front door and turned right and left before twirling completely around. Peter did a double-take. "Wow!"

"Close your mouth, dear," she said. "You're gaping."

"Ma, you're quite a sight. And I mean that in the best possible way."

"So, you like my new look?"

"Like it? I love it." He gave her a quick hug. "I thought we'd drive north along Ocean Boulevard, watch the sun go down and enjoy some great local seafood."

"Sounds wonderful, let's go."

During the drive to Manalapan, Theresa bombarded Peter with questions about Amy. He did his best to answer without revealing too much information.

"Why are you so reluctant to discuss your relationship?" she asked. "It's obvious you have strong feelings for this woman. Your face lights up every time you mention her name."

"Ma, you're imagining things."

"Why can't you admit that the two of you have a *thing* going on?"

"Okay, you're right. I think she's the kind of gal I could settle down with."

"Hah! I knew it. A mother senses these things."

"Now can we drop the subject and talk about something else?"

"As a matter of fact, I have some good news. I'm thinking of selling the house up north and moving to Villa Paraiso."

The car swerved.

"Watch it, kiddo," Theresa said. "You've got precious cargo sitting next to you."

Peter gripped the steering wheel tighter. "Whoa. When did you make that decision?"

"I recognize a good thing when I see it."

Peter pulled up to the valet in front of an impressive, two-story wooden structure with outdoor seating on both levels. They exited the car and Theresa hooked her arm around Peter's elbow. She pointed toward the sun low in the sky. "I've never seen a more beautiful sight. Have you been here with Amy?"

"Ma, that's enough with the romance."

"Love you, Pumpkin," she said.

Peter said, "I love you too. And Ma?"

"Yes, dear?"

"I'm glad you decided to move down... and there's something else."

"What's that?"

"You look terrific."

SIXTY-SEVEN

THE PLACARD IN THE DOOR'S Lucite sign holder read "class in session." A group of women wearing too many jangling bracelets gathered near the dance floor. Several men stood nearby looking like they'd rather be anywhere else but there. *La Cumparsita's* distinctive Latin beat echoed throughout the room.

Mary and Jane peered through the partially open door. "Looks like a small group, a few couples and Bunny," Jane said.

Mary rolled her eyes. "It doesn't matter how many people show up. Charles isn't paid by the piece, no pun intended."

Jane stifled a giggle.

Charles glanced up at the clock mounted on the wall above the door and crooked his finger. "Come, come, ladies, you're late again. We've got a lot to cover today. I want to wrap up the Café Tango and move on to something more sensual, the Argentine Tango."

Jane pushed open the door. "Guess we're stuck with each other," she said, loud enough for Charles to hear. "We should look great doing the Argentine together."

"You know," he said, "I rotate in and out so all the single ladies have an opportunity to practice with a male partner."

Jane whispered in Mary's ear, "I wonder who he's rotating

in and out of now that Vicky's back in the sack with her husband?"

Charles clapped his hands to get their attention. "We're here to dance. If you ladies would rather chit-chat, I suggest you step outside."

One of the men called out, "Can we get going? It's enough that my wife dragged me here and made me wear these damn dress shoes. Now we're standing around not doing anything and you're wasting more time mouthing off to the ladies."

Charles walked up to the man. "Hold on a minute, buddy."

The man shook his fist and said, "I'd like to show *you* a step or two."

His wife grabbed his arm. "Honey, please, calm down."

The other women glared at Mary and Jane.

One woman waived her finger in their faces. "See what you've started. Where's your consideration for the rest of us who *really* want to learn tango?"

Mary moved closer. "What exactly do you mean by that crack?"

Charles put up his hand. "Cut it out, you two. We seem to have started off on the wrong foot and for that I apologize. It sounds like everybody's a little on edge today."

"We all have an off day once in a while," Bunny said.

"Thanks, Bunny," Charles said. "I appreciate your support."

The man who initiated the altercation threw up his hands. "I'm done. I've had it." He took his wife by the elbow and ushered her across the floor and out the door.

Charles shook his head. "Sorry, guys. I doubt we'll get anything accomplished today. I think it's best if we cancel class and resume next week at our regular time."

The grumbling died down and everyone except Bunny picked up their belongings and exited the room.

Bunny watched Charles stuff CD's into a canvas bag.

"I make a mean coffee cake," she said, "and I just happen to have one cooling on my kitchen counter." She blushed slightly as she recalled that after she found out that Charles was no longer *shtupping* Vicky, she'd fantasized that he had ravaged *her* on that same countertop.

Charles turned and smiled. "Does it have cinnamon crumbles on top?"

"Lots and lots."

"A nice piece of homemade cake and a cup of coffee sounds great. Got any decaf?"

"Sure do."

"Then what are we waiting for?" He motioned for her to lead the way.

* * *

Bunny parked in her driveway and waited for Charles. He had always shown her the utmost respect when they'd partnered during dance class, but now she felt apprehensive. Too many years had passed without the physical closeness of a man.

She picked at her cuticles. When she looked up, Charles was standing beside her car. He opened the door and helped her out. She fumbled for her house keys. He leaned over and steadied her hand. They entered her tastefully decorated living-dining area. Charles let out a long whistle.

"You approve?" she said.

"I sure do," he answered. "I especially like the little doo-dads and doo-hickeys."

"It's just a little of this and a little of that all thrown together. I brought some of the furniture with me, but the rest I filled in. The consignment shops down here are wonderful."

"I've passed a few, but never taken the time to visit one."

"You don't know what you're missing," she said. "Oh, I do ramble on when I'm nervous. I don't entertain much."

"Then I'm truly honored."

Bunny gestured toward the wicker table and chairs in the breakfast nook. "Make yourself at home. You did say decaf, didn't you?"

"Yes, if that's not a problem."

"No problem. I start my day with regular. Gives my brain a jolt, but then I switch to decaf."

Charles winked. "What a coincidence. I do the same thing. Wonder what else we have in common."

Bunny's pulse raced. *I've been out of the dating arena for so long I've forgotten how to act. Just serve the damn coffee and cake.* She busied herself searching in a drawer for the cake cutter.

Charles startled her. "Need any help?" He stood close enough for Bunny to feel his breath on the back of her neck.

She turned to face him. "I'm... I'm good."

"Are you?" Charles took the cake cutter from her hand and placed it on the counter.

"I... I need some water," she said.

"And what else do you need?" Charles whispered.

No response.

"What you need is to feel alive inside." He grabbed her buttocks with both hands and lifted her up onto the countertop. "You can't tell me that you haven't imagined what it would be like to make love together."

Bunny tried to protest, but Charles covered her mouth with his own. He placed his hand on her chest.

She flinched. "I... my breasts... I don't have—"

He kissed her gently and unbuttoned her blouse. His lips brushed the void where flesh had once defined her. "It's you that I want, not your damn breasts."

His warm, moist tongue against her skin sent shivers down her spine. She leaned back on her elbows and moaned as she surrendered body and soul.

SIXTY-EIGHT

ONE MORNING EACH WEEK, six members of the Men's Club met for breakfast at Lido Terrace, the informal poolside café. Popular Broadway showtunes played softly in the background. The group sat at their favorite table and ordered the Breakfast Special: oatmeal or grits, two eggs fried or scrambled, home fried potatoes or tomatoes, bagel or toast, accompanied by endless cups of coffee. Breakfast meats were available for an additional charge and Al Frank always added a double order.

Burt Rosen's mouth watered as he watched Al bite into a sausage, lick his fingers, and smack his lips. "Boy, do I envy you," Burt said. "There'd be hell to pay if my wife smells grease on my breath. Aren't you worried about your LDL?"

Al took another bite from the spicy breakfast meat held between his stubby fingers. "I really shouldn't, but sausage is a lot like sex."

"How so?"

"Too much of either one will kill you, but what a way to go."

"You've got that right," John Taylor said.

Burt extracted a pull-out section from the *Sun Sentinel.* "Fort Lauderdale International Boat Show's opening next month. Anyone interested?"

"A few years ago, I was in town for a Law Enforcement Conference," Ed Marrone said. "After I viewed the exhibits, I was down in the dumps for days."

"You're kidding."

"I'm not kidding," Ed said. "I'm dead serious."

Al stopped shoveling scrambled eggs into his mouth. "Boat show, down in the dumps. I don't get the connection."

"Same thing happened to me," John said. "I realized there's no way in hell I can afford one of those *superyachts.* Upkeep alone is ten percent of the purchase price."

Jay Friedlander busied himself with his iPad. "Here's a company that leases boats for a day or even for a few hours. We can all chip in and—"

"Lease what, a dinghy?" Ed asked.

"I thought it sounded like a good idea," Jay whined.

"Let's see what else is going on in the world." Burt thumbed through the main section. "The National Debt is out of control with no sign of recovering anytime soon and terrorists are everywhere. That wall that cost the U.S. a gazillion dollars is crumbling. Border Patrol discovered another tunnel between Mexico and the U.S. Otherwise, we're in great shape."

"Yeah, sure we are," Ed muttered under his breath.

Burt folded the news section and placed it under the neat pile at the side of his plate. He skimmed through the Travel and Leisure section. Then he said, "You guys won't believe this."

"Believe what?" Jay asked.

Burt continued reading to himself.

Al stopped squeezing ketchup onto his plate. "Hey, Burt, what gives?"

"Ever hear of a *nudie* cruise?"

"You're shittin' us," Al said.

"It's right here in black and white," Burt said. "The group that runs them is celebrating their thirtieth season."

Al frowned. "Where've I been all this time?"

"They have themed cruises for everything else," John said. "I actually worked with a guy whose family vacationed at a nudist camp every year."

"Did you say Buddhist or nudist?" Jay asked.

"Nudist."

Several people at nearby tables turned to stare.

Jay grimaced and said, "Thanks for the clarification, but the whole thing creeps me out."

"I don't know," Al said. "I wouldn't mind refereeing the women's volleyball games."

Rick Gould sat quietly nursing a hangover and a dull ache in his lower back, a result of scoring at Artie's on the Bay the previous night. After verbally sparring with a psycho-babble chick for most of the evening, he'd finally gotten into her panties in the back-seat of his car. He had little interest in this morning's current events until he'd heard *nudie cruise.* "Hey guys," he said, "I've got a great idea."

Burt gasped, "Hey, he's alive."

"Wiseass, forget the boat show. Any of you up for a nudie cruise?

"You want to get us married guys killed?" Burt said. He turned to the next page and held up his hand. "Whoa! What's this? One of Hollywood's biggest box office draws announced that she's having sex reassignment surgery."

"What?" Al reached over and tried to grab the newspaper.

Burt pulled it back, took a sip of coffee, and rose to leave. "Can't be late for my spa appointment."

"You're not serious, are you?" Ed asked.

"The hell with the spa," Rick said. "You can't leave without telling us who's having the sex-change surgery."

Burt tucked the folded newspaper under his arm. "Sorry, gotta go."

Ed pushed back his chair, kicked off his pool shoes and inspected his toes. He put his hand to his mouth and nibbled a hangnail. "Vicky's been after me to get a manicure and pedicure."

"Now, I've heard it all," John said. "See you guys next week."

Rick was the last one left at the table. He searched for the latest transgender news on his iPhone until something in his peripheral vision caught his attention. He reached over and scooped up the small piece of sausage that remained on Al's plate, and popped it into his mouth.

SIXTY-NINE

DR. BENNETT AND HECTOR sat opposite each other with their knees almost touching. A yellow pad resting on her lap slid to the floor. She bent to retrieve it. Her bare leg brushed against Hector's pants leg. For a moment, his gaze locked onto hers. He wriggled back in his seat and cupped his hands over his groin.

The sexual tension in the room was palpable.

Dr. Bennett pushed her chair back. *Maybe I'll drop by Artie's,* she thought. *I sure wouldn't mind bumping into that retired dentist again, but for now, it's back to business.* "When you peer through windows," she asked, "are you sexually aroused?"

Hector squirmed in his seat. "What kinda monster you think I am?"

"I don't know. You tell me. Do you think you're a monster?"

He slammed his hands down on the armrests and raised himself up off the chair. "I no monster."

"Whenever you experience these urges, do you feel helpless, like when you were a boy?"

Hector settled back in his chair.

She went on, "Are you afraid you'll become an abuser

like your father, someone who rages and takes advantage of helpless women?"

Hector shrugged. "Don' know."

"During your childhood, you witnessed traumatic events that were no doubt upsetting to a young boy." Dr. Bennett lowered her voice. "You did whatever you could to protect your mother. Your presence must have been a comfort to her."

Hector took a deep breath. "I hope is true."

"The person you are today isn't only shaped by events from the past. Often, our behavior, the way we act, is influenced by fear or stress we experience in the present."

Hector flexed his biceps. "Hector strong… fear nothin'… nobody."

"Nobody?"

He smiled. "Jus' you."

"Why is that?"

"You doctor, you smart. You know stuff Hector don' know."

"I'm not the only smart one in this room. It's not about education. You have to be smart to figure out how to survive. Whether you realize it or not, you've developed habits to help you deal with stressful situations. Our goal is for you to have a satisfying life in a more acceptable way."

"I pray this is so," Hector said.

Dr. Bennett leaned forward. "From time-to-time you may feel nervous or anxious and return to your old ways, but don't worry. A little slip is not a failure. You can do this. I know you can."

Hector shook his head. "I no sure. I worry all day, all night. I no legal in this country. Sí, I have papers, but…" He whispered, "Papers I buy from stranger."

"The pathway to citizenship is in a state of flux, but laws are changing all the time. It's possible that it won't be long before undocumented Mexican Nationals will have the opportunity to apply for permanent residency. You won't have to worry about Immigration and Customs Enforcement agents breaking down your door in the middle of the night."

His face flushed. *"Politicos* say lotta stuff they no mean."

"That's true, but you owe it to yourself to remain hopeful."

"Your *Señora Presidenta* has more to worry about than Hector. You think she care 'bout me?'"

"How long have you been in this country?"

Hector scratched his head. "No' sure. Long time."

"You're ahead of the game. You speak English and you're employed. Hopefully you don't have a criminal record because peeping through people's windows is more than a nuisance sexual offense. If you're caught, you'll be arrested and possibly deported. You don't want that to happen, do you?"

"No."

"You're well on your way to becoming the person you want to be. You work hard, you have the love of a good woman, and you've reached out for help. Change won't come easy, but you'll see. In the end it will be worth the effort."

Hector stared straight ahead.

Dr. Bennett sighed, "I think this is a good place for us to stop."

* * *

After Hector left, Dr. Bennett wondered if she had offered him false hope. *Am I fueling his anxiety? Peeping Toms are more dangerous than people realize and so much depends on the therapeutic process.*

She rose from her chair and ran her fingers across several shelves filled with reference books until her hand came to rest on the DSM-5, the mental health professional's Bible. She thumbed through the pages until she found what she was searching for.

Paraphilia: a condition in which a person's sexual arousal and gratification depend on fantasizing about and engaging in sexual behavior that is atypical. Characterized by abnormal sexual behavior or uninhibited sexual fantasies and urges that keep him coming back or seeking new outlets for his fantasies.

She replaced the book on the shelf and returned to her chair. *Is there more to Hector than meets the eye? I hope I'm not playing with fire.*

SEVENTY

ALLISON SCRUBBED HER FACE with a soapy washcloth until her complexion glowed. She leaned into the mirror and searched for pesky fine lines destined to become deep-set wrinkles.

A whimsical wooden plaque dangled from a golden ribbon above the towel rack, a reminder of the inevitable. The plaque pictured a woman seated at a dressing table, staring at her reflection in the mirror. The caption underneath read:

> *Mirror, mirror, on the wall...*
> *What the *#?@&! happened?*

She drenched her face in moisturizer and rummaged through her cosmetic bag. After applying concealer, blush, eye liner, and eye shadow, she dug deeper in search of mascara that promised to lengthen and thicken eyelashes. She scrutinized a blood red, long-lasting lipstick. Usually, a pale-pink lip gloss sufficed, but tonight was different. A hunting expedition required specific accoutrements.

She misted her body from head to toe and everywhere in-between with *J'adore,* before pulling on a leopard-print thong and fastening a matching push-up bra. She shook out her hair and tamed a few wild strands with hairspray.

Allison zipped up her *little black dress*. The mirror over the vanity revealed a silhouette that had changed dramatically since the last time she'd worn it. Her *derriere* didn't yet qualify for admission into the Kardashian clan, but if she didn't start exercising soon that was a definite possibility.

She took one last look in the mirror and recoiled. *You look like you're going to a Halloween party.* She tore off a piece of toilet tissue, vigorously rubbed her cheeks and toned down the vibrant lip color with her pale-pink standby. She tugged at her dress and adjusted her breasts, which had risen to splendid proportions. "There, that's better," she said to herself. "Artie's on the Bay, watch out. Here I come."

* * *

By the time Allison arrived at the legendary meet market, the parking lot was filled to capacity. The latest model cars, interspersed with older models destined for the scrap heap, were indicative of the diverse singles mingling inside. She circled around twice before she relinquished her BMW to the parking attendant.

Inside the frigid vestibule, the throbbing bass blasted through the sound system accompanied by synchronized mood lighting. The entry doors slid open and a trio of women in their mid-to-late thirties brushed past her. She watched as a considerably older woman, wearing too much makeup and fragrance, followed at a snail's pace, her windswept facial features the result of an overzealous cosmetic surgeon.

What the hell am I doing here? Allison thought to herself. *I could be home with a glass of Chardonnay in one hand and my trusty Rabbit, guaranteed to please, in the other.*

A short, balding man with an impish grin reached from behind Allison and gently touched her elbow. She spun around and, for a split second, imagined Hector standing there.

"Don't think too long about going inside," he said. "You may lose your nerve. Anyway, what's the worst thing that can happen? A guy like me asks you to dance?" He entered the cavernous room and shouted over his shoulder, "Good luck! Save a dance for me!"

Before Allison had a chance to respond, he'd disappeared into the crowd milling around inside.

Allison shrugged. *Nothing ventured, nothing gained.*

She strolled past the bouncer carding a group of underage girls attempting to gain entry with forged ID's.

The bouncer raised his head, smiled at Allison, and nodded his approval.

SEVENTY-ONE

THROUGHOUT HIS WORKDAY, Hector struggled to push Dr. Bennett from his thoughts. Each time he replayed the moment her bare leg brushed against his, his body tingled with excitement.

Seated on his bed at the end of the day, he forced down leftover rice and beans. In between bites, he sipped beer and stared into the darkness through the grungy window at the foot of his bed. The tingling sensation in his groin returned. His gaze turned toward heaven. He beseeched God to forgive him for what he had become and for the feelings he had been struggling with all day. He placed the half-empty plate on the dresser, put on his cap, and hurried to his car.

The security guard on duty at Villa Paraiso's front gate accepted Hector's mumbled excuse for the reason he'd returned to the maintenance building after dark.

"I go home, no wallet. I leave in locker," he said and slapped his forehead. *"Estúpido!"*

The guard waved him through.

Hector followed the road to Dr. Bennett's villa and parked in the shadows. He crouched low and edged his way along the shrubbery until he came to a window. He raised his head just enough to see that the curtains were drawn.

He slid along the wall and stared into another darkened window, but there was no sign of Dr. Bennett. Consumed with guilt and shame, he retreated.

On the way to his car, fragrant blossoms and trilling birds reminded him of the peace and tranquility that eluded him. He longed for his home and the taste of his *mamacita's* sweet rolls.

SEVENTY-TWO

BEVERLY PRETENDED TO BE ASLEEP until Jay had left for his weekly golf outing with his recently retired Board of Education buddies from up north. She would have preferred to stay in bed the rest of the day, but recently Jay had insisted she get out of her rut. Except for the Women's Club meetings, she wasn't interested in attending lectures she couldn't care less about, or playing cards or mahjong. She believed that women immersed themselves in mind-numbing activities in an attempt to stave off the hollowness of their unfulfilled lives. She never considered the possibility that she was becoming one of those women.

To appease Jay, she had scheduled a 9 a.m. appointment at the spa. An aesthetician would no doubt slather her with oils and exfoliating cream, encase her body in a seaweed wrap, and after a facial, end with a manicure and pedicure. Thinking about the morning ahead exhausted her.

* * *

Jay returned home to find Beverly slouched on a patio chair with her bare feet resting on an ottoman. An unopened magazine lay on the floor beside her. The overhead fan turned lazily. Jay adjusted the speed to "high."

Beverly shielded her hair with her hands. "Turn that damn thing down. It was fine the way it was."

Jay rolled his eyes and adjusted the speed. "You need to make an effort to get out of the house. If you're not feeling well, maybe you should see a doctor."

Beverly wasn't in the mood to explain that she had devoted the entire morning to a Deluxe Spa Package where she was pampered like a thoroughbred and still felt like crap. "It's nothing. Really, I'm fine."

"You're not fine," Jay said. "You should see the forlorn look on your face. You mope around here all day, and that's when you're not napping."

"I wasn't napping."

"And when was the last time we attended a show or had dinner with another couple?"

"Please, just leave me alone," she said.

"Believe me, I've tried, but your behavior's beginning to affect me and our marriage."

"I never stop you from doing anything."

"That's not the point, Bev. I'm worried about you."

"You don't get it do you? This isn't about us."

Jay frowned. "What do you mean, not about us? What am I missing here?"

Beverly rose from the chair and averted her eyes. "You wouldn't understand."

"Try me."

She faced Jay and stifled a sob. "Most nights after you're asleep, I sit in the dark bathroom for hours crying. I can't stop thinking about our precious child. She doesn't deserve to be punished for *our* sins. I'd give anything for her to have a normal life."

Jay's voice cracked. "I'd give anything, too."

"I miss her terribly," Beverly said.

"You can't be serious. We haven't been down here that long. Besides, when we were home we rarely visited her except on birthdays, Christmas, and an occasional Sunday."

Beverly glared at Jay and clenched her fists until her nails dug into her palms. "Home, home," she said, in a shrill voice. "We had to run away from our home, remember?"

"I don't know what I can say or do to make things better."

Beverly shrugged. "There's nothing you can say, but I can tell you this, not a day goes by that I don't regret sending her away. We abandoned her."

"Abandoned her?" Jay shook his head. "No way. We thought long and hard before we made the decision about a residential facility."

"Maybe so, but every month when *I* open the statement I feel as if my heart is wrenched from my chest. The emotional pain is excruciating."

"And you think I don't feel pain?"

"It's not the same for you."

"How can you say such a thing?"

"*I* gave birth to her."

"That's a low blow."

"Sorry, but it's true."

"Why didn't you say something sooner?"

Beverly stared directly into Jay's eyes. "I'm telling you now. I've made a decision."

"Oh," he said, as he dropped like a sack of garbage into the chair opposite Beverly. The rattan frame creaked in protest.

"I'm moving back to New York to be near our daughter."

"Just like that?" he said. "No discussion?"

"There's nothing to discuss. My mind's made up."

"Where does that leave me?"

"I'm not sure, but I know I need to do this... alone."

"Why don't we try to find a place for her down here?"

"I've done the research and nothing compares to Mayfair."

"Where will you stay?"

"With my parents."

Jay shrugged. "You're not going to visit every day. What will you do the rest of the time?"

"I'll find work."

"Sounds like you've been planning this for awhile."

"Please understand, I can't go on like this," she said. "It's not good for either of us or for our—"

"Damn it, say her name! *Debbie.* Our daughter's name is Debbie."

"Sorry. Debbie."

"She's mine, too, you know."

"You have two other children. If anything happens to *my* child, I have nothing."

SEVENTY-THREE

MOST NIGHTS JOHN DOZED OFF only to awaken a few minutes later. All attempts to relieve his insomnia proved unsuccessful. More often than not, he found himself slumped over the kitchen sink retching.

Memories of horrific events from his tour of duty in Nam plagued him, his comrades in arms on foot patrol, their shattered bones, dismembered bodies and blood spurting from severed arteries. Soul-piercing shrieks alternated with, "John, don't leave me like this. I beg you… please… *shoot me.*"

John and Claudia watched the eleven o'clock news from their bed. A report of a suicide bombing in a busy marketplace, not far from Baghdad, filled the television screen with gory scenes straight out of a horror movie. A heart-wrenching update on a previous newscast followed. Another young child in Central Florida, this time an Asian girl, had been kidnapped and brutally assaulted before she was murdered. Campers had discovered her mutilated body.

Visions of the dead girl and the suicide bombing intermingled with John's flashbacks of Ng. Questions flooded his thoughts. What if that had been our child? Why hadn't he and Claudia had children? Why had he refused to accompany her to a fertility specialist or consider adoption? Was it his ego that wouldn't allow him to explore other options, his college jock persona, or the guilt he felt for abandoning the child he had helped conceive in Nam? Was he a sham, a miserable imitation of a *real* man, not the warrior he imagined himself to be?

Before he'd drifted off to sleep, he rolled over and cupped Claudia's breast with his hand. She moaned, reached behind her, and gently stroked his penis.

* * *

The following morning, John rubbed sleep from his eyes and tried to make sense of the dream he'd had shortly before he awakened. A young man dressed in Army fatigues had stood silhouetted against a pastoral landscape. A few yards away, a woman suckled a child, humming softly. She lifted her head and smiled at the man before she turned and walked a few steps. She stopped and looked back, waved goodbye, and continued across the pasture toward a distant hillside.

John experienced a moment of clarity. *What's done is done.* He had to stop beating himself up over the past. He kissed the nape of Claudia's neck.

She rolled over and pulled him close.

A tear rolled down his cheek. He felt blessed to have this wonderful, understanding woman beside him.

SEVENTY-FOUR

ANGELA WAS HOPING she wouldn't have to spend another evening alone. "Are you sure you won't stay up and watch the Red Carpet Special?" she asked Beth. "The show's been advertised all week. Facelifts, fashionistas… It sounds like fun."

Beth pushed her chair back from the dinner table. "No thanks. I'm pooped. Good night."

"Are you coming down with something?" Angela reached over. "Let me feel your forehead."

Beth pulled away. "I just don't feel up to it. Bed's the best place for me."

"We don't have to watch TV. We can play cards, or talk, or—"

"I appreciate your concern. Really, I do, but I wouldn't be good company. I'm sure I'll feel better in the morning."

"I hope so. Tell you what. I'll make your favorite breakfast, French toast. How does that sound?"

Beth shrugged. "It's up to you."

"If you like, I'll make pancakes instead."

"Makes no difference, whichever is easier."

Beth stood up and headed toward the hallway leading to

their bedrooms. She called over her shoulder, "Thank you for everything. You've been a good friend."

A sense of foreboding sent a chill along Angela's spine. In recent months, Beth had become withdrawn and often refused to accompany her to social events or shopping outings.

"Good night dear. Sleep well. You'll be in my prayers, as always.

* * *

Angela looked over at the rooster clock above the pantry door and said aloud, "Eight-forty." There was no need to wake Beth until the French toast was stacked on a serving platter in the center of the table dusted with powdered sugar, just the way she liked it.

Angela lined up the ingredients for French toast on the countertop and cut crusts off six slices of whole wheat bread. She beat eggs, cinnamon, and vanilla into frothy peaks, slid a generous pat of butter into a large frying pan and melted it over low heat. She dipped the slices into the fragrant mixture and in between sips of almond milk, turned the French toast with a spatula until each piece was golden brown.

Her stomach growled at the exact moment the rooster clock crowed.

"It's nine o'clock, Beth! Everything's ready and I'm *starving.*"

Several minutes passed.

Angela hurried down the hallway and knocked on Beth's bedroom door.

No answer.

She knocked again and slowly opened the door. An unnatural stillness enveloped the room.

Beth's face was turned away, a light-weight cover wrapped around her.

Angela moved closer. "Beth dear, you're scaring me. Please, wake up."

No response.

Angela struggled to pull down the cover and placed two fingers on the side of Beth's neck in search of a pulse. Her skin felt eerily cool to the touch.

A sob hitched in Angela's throat. She hurried to the other side of the bed and stumbled over two empty prescription bottles scattered across the carpet.

The reality of the moment touched her like an ice-cold hand on her heart. She fumbled for the phone on the nightstand and punched in 9-1-1.

The operator assured her that help was on the way.

Angela reached over and took Beth's lifeless hand in hers. *If only I'd done more.* She fell to her knees and wailed like a wounded animal. Her agonizing cry continued until her throat felt as ragged as her shattered heart.

SEVENTY-FIVE

ANGELA HAD CHOSEN ST. ANN'S Roman Catholic Church, fifty miles north of Boca, hoping to avoid meeting anyone from Villa Paraiso. She hesitated in the doorway before she dipped her fingers in holy water and made the sign of the cross. She stopped half-way down the center aisle, genuflected, and entered an empty pew.

She inhaled the familiar scent of incense and was reminded how long it had been since she had attended a church service. Now, sitting in God's house without Beth, she felt like a hypocrite. The iconic statues and splendid stained glass depicting the Stations of the Cross did little to comfort her.

Following Beth's death, she had been riddled with guilt. Beth's parents had graciously absolved her of responsibility, but she was unable to forgive herself. She should have reported her despondent friend's deteriorating mental condition. She never should have gone to bed that last night without checking on Beth.

A family with two young boys entered the pew and sat down next to Angela. The woman lowered the kneeler and whispered to her boys. The family knelt to pray.

Angela knelt beside them and felt the soft padding on her knees. *Almighty God, I remember before you today your faithful servant Beth; and I pray that, having opened to her the gates of larger life, you will receive her into your joyful service, that, with all who have faithfully served you in the past, she may share in the eternal victory of Jesus Christ our Lord. Amen.*

Father Simon stepped to the pulpit and welcomed his congregants in a booming, baritone voice that resonated throughout the chapel. A rousing hymn, led by the choir master, followed.

Angela chose to mouth the words. She ignored out-stretched hands during the Sign of the Cross and remained in her seat during Holy Communion. She kept her head bowed during Scripture readings.

Father Simon recited the benediction and concluded his sermon, "In the name of the Father, and the Son, and of the Holy Spirit."

For the first time, Angela understood the real reason she had been drawn to a house of worship after a long absence. She not only hoped to pray for Beth's soul, she sought solace for herself. The family seated next to her rose to leave. Angela followed them out.

Father Simon waited outside the church entrance and greeted his congregants. When it was Angela's turn, he took both her hands in his. Instead of his standard salutation, "Thank you for coming," he squeezed her hands and said, "I hope to see you next Sunday."

"I…"

Father Simon's intense hazel eyes riveted Angela's gaze. "You will come again, won't you?"

This is where I belong, she thought. "Yes, Father. I promise I'll be back next week. And Father, thank you and praise be to God."

She took a deep breath. The heaviness in her chest, the constant reminder of her dearest friend's passing, was no longer there.

SEVENTY-SIX

A WIND-UP ALARM CLOCK sat on the chair next to Hector's bed, along with the scarred, plastic radio he had purchased at a local thrift shop. The clock's glow-in-the-dark hands indicated 5:10 a.m. He sat up in bed, stretched his arms, and stifled a yawn.

He reached under the chair and retrieved the empty milk carton he used as a urinal in case the bathroom down the hall was occupied. He sighed as urine rushed against the inside of the carton like a raging river during a storm. Then he fumbled with the radio dials in search of a static-free frequency, but all he heard was *buzz*. Out of frustration, he banged the radio against the chair. The signal came in loud and clear.

The local station's co-anchors bantered back-and-forth, commenting on human interest stories. That was followed by the female newscaster describing the latest technology used to detect tropical storms, before they become full-blown hurricanes. "The National Hurricane Center has announced this year's forecasts will be more accurate than ever before…"

"What's different about this year?" another radio voice asked.

"The NHC has two new sophisticated supercomputers that boost forecasting accuracy. These computers have the capability of performing at a mind-boggling 1.5 quadrillion operations per second."

"1.5 quadrillion operations per second?"

"Amazing, isn't it?" the radio woman said. "And the opportunity to be dazzled by their performance could arrive a lot sooner than we think."

"Sounds like you have a little surprise in store for our listeners."

"Unfortunately, I do. Our hurricane season usually runs from June through November, but with the help of these supercomputers, NHC has predicted not only an early hurricane season, but an exceptionally active one as well."

"Hear that folks? You need to start thinking about what to do before, during and—"

Pounding on Hector's door drowned out the broadcast. A man's voice said, "Man, is too early for that shit. Turn that fuckin' thing down."

Hector wasn't in the mood to confront the surly tenant on the other side of the door. He turned off the radio and lifted his cherished crucifix to his lips. *"Padre,* please, I beg you, for me and for Rosa and for Villa Paraiso, keep us safe from hurricane and no lemme open door to *estúpido."*

A door down the hall slammed shut.

"Gracias, Padre," Hector said.

SEVENTY-SEVEN

PETER FOLLOWED THE HURRICANE updates and listened for confirmation that a direct hit from the season's first named hurricane, Arial, was imminent. Her outer bands—unexpected wind gusts and torrential rain—were a preview of what was to come.

Peter put his contingency plan into action the moment the hurricane watch was announced. He ordered the outdoor areas secured, pool chairs and tables stored away, and loose palm fronds collected. Non-essential personnel were sent home. He arranged to remain on-site in his mother's villa and insisted Amy and her son, Michael, join them.

Peter toured the entire property twice before he felt confident Villa Paraiso was ready to withstand its first hurricane. He grabbed a change of clothes and a Maglite from his office and headed over to the model villa where his mother was staying. He watched as she stuffed non-perishable foods into green shopping sacks. "Are you sure I'm not forcing you out, Ma?"

Theresa held a box of pita chips in one hand and a cellophane bag of shelled walnuts in the other. "Not at all dear, Emily and Peggy and I are looking forward to spending some girl time together. And since Emily's villa has more room, we're staying over at her place. Besides, you and Amy and the boy will have more privacy without me underfoot."

"I know you, Ma. You think after I play house with Amy and her son you'll end up with a new family."

"You believe your mother is that devious?"

"Not my mother." Peter planted a huge kiss on her cheek. "Come on, Ma. Let's get this stuff in the car before this freakin' storm arrives."

"Peter!"

"Sorry, Ma, but this whole situation's making me nuts. As of now the hurricane is considered a Category One tropical storm, but by the time it makes landfall it's expected to increase to a Category Two or higher."

"Is there a big difference?"

"You'd be surprised at the damage one-hundred and ten mile-per-hour winds can cause, compared to only ninety-five. At the max, we're talking trees uprooted and blown away, downed power poles, coastal properties destroyed and with a storm surge, flooding up to eight miles inland. At the least, moderate damage to structures and roofing and a few trees down, but no flooding."

"What are you, a meteorologist? How do you know all this?"

"You have to be aware of these things if you live down here."

"You're scaring me, Peter."

"I don't mean to, but you should be prepared in the event that—"

"I'm excited about our fun pajama party. I'd rather not concern myself with hurricane categories. Makes my head spin. Besides, ignorance is bliss."

"I hope you have a supply of candles and a flashlight for this fun party of yours and plenty of bottled water."

"Emily has candles and water, but I'm not sure about a flashlight."

"I've got an extra one in my car." Peter grabbed a bag in each hand and hugged a third one to his chest. "Do you think you have enough food here?"

"Well, it is a party and we don't know how long the hurricane will last."

Peter shrugged. *Maybe ignorance is bliss.*

Theresa grasped the handle on her overnight bag and followed Peter out to his car.

SEVENTY-EIGHT

HURRICANE ARIAL MOVED RAPIDLY across Palm Beach County, exactly as the forecast had predicted. By 2:30 a.m., the eye of the storm hovered directly over Boca Raton.

Peter stood with his face pressed against the living room window, the eerie calm a welcome relief from the endless hours Arial had hammered the windows and rooftops. At one point during the night he feared the high impact glass, guaranteed to withstand 150 mph gusts, wouldn't survive the storm's intensity. Debris had glanced off windows before it was carried away by howling winds. Whenever he heard a loud noise, he darted from room-to-room to check on ceilings and wall joints for signs of water leakage.

At the height of the storm he had checked on Amy and Michael and found them sleeping soundly. He found it hard to believe that a few hours earlier the boy had been paralyzed with fear.

Michael had almost knocked Amy off her chair when he grabbed her around the neck. "Mommy! Mommy! I don't like the dark."

"Michael, it's okay," she'd said. "I'm here with you and Peter's here. You'll protect us, won't you, Peter?"

Peter had spoken in an authoritative tone. "Of course, I will, but this is a two-man job. Michael, can I count on you to help me out?"

The boy gazed up at his mother.

Amy gave him a gentle nudge. "Go on, babe."

He tugged at her sleeve. "Come with me."

"I have my job, taking care of the two of you. Peter really needs your help."

Peter came around the table and took the child's small hand in his.

"It's important that we check all the rooms to make sure they're dry. You wouldn't want to sleep on a soggy mattress now, would you?"

Michael giggled, "Nooo."

"Tell you what, after we're finished, how about a reward? I bet if we do a good job, your mom will let us have a couple of those devils food cookies I've had my eye on."

Michael giggled again and squeezed Peter's hand. "I love milk and cookies."

"Then what are we waiting for? Let's get started."

* * *

For most of the night, Peter stayed in the living room on high alert. He passed the time recalling how he had always welcomed a challenge. He was no slouch when it came to responsibility, but lately he wasn't sure he was up to the task. He considered the possibility he might be entering the "stop and smell the roses" phase of life.

On quiet Sunday afternoons, he had often kicked back with a glass of booze in his Brooklyn office. Thinking about it now triggered his desire to replicate the good old days.

The beam from his Maglite bounced off the toaster oven, the blender, and a George Foreman grill before he spotted what he was searching for. *Leave it to my mother to hide a bottle of Italian Red behind the paper towel holder.*

He carried the half-empty bottle and a wine glass back to the living room, sunk into the couch, and put his bare feet up on the coffee table. He eased the cork from the bottle and filled his glass. He took a long drink of the full-bodied Lambrusco and sighed.

I think I'm beginning to smell the roses.

SEVENTY-NINE

SHORTLY BEFORE DAWN, Arial turned and roared up the Eastern Seaboard toward the Carolinas. Gusty winds accompanied by broad rain bands continued to pound Florida's coastline, but Boca Raton was in the clear. The area had sustained minimal damage, with the exception of minor flooding east of Federal Highway. Many communities were without power.

Grids that supplied electricity to hospitals, police, fire stations, and major roadways were restored first. The rest of the customers had to wait their turn. Businesses along the Florida Turnpike were worth their weight in gold. After long blackouts, predictably, locals always headed in that direction in search of hot food and freshly brewed coffee.

* * *

Amy and Michael were still asleep when Peter slipped out of the villa. The smell of damp earth filled his nostrils. He made a quick tour of the entire property, where he found a few torn screened patio enclosures, small trees uprooted, and a handful of roof tiles scattered about. A skeleton maintenance crew was out loading debris onto dump trucks.

Peter was pleasantly surprised to find two people on duty at the guardhouse: Mac, a tough old bird who never missed a shift, and a pleasant looking woman with steel grey hair piled high on her head, standing at his side.

"Mornin', Mr. Duke," Mac said. "Hope you don't mind, I brought the missus with me."

"Mac, I'm so glad to see you, I wouldn't care if you brought a marching band with you."

Mac's wife's face lit up. "Wild horses couldn't keep him away."

"I know what you mean," Peter said." He's a good man." Peter's stomach growled. "I'm on my way over to the bagel place near the turnpike. If it's up and running can I bring you back anything?"

"I don't wanna trouble you," Mac said.

His wife chimed in. "That'd be real nice of you. Two coffees light and sweet, please."

Peter saluted. "Yes, ma'am. Two coffees it is."

Peter drove as if he were navigating a mine field. Roads leading to the turnpike were strewn with debris and standing water reaching halfway up the car's tires. Without working traffic lights, motorists were forced to slow down and yield at intersections. The drive took three times longer than usual, but he arrived at his destination without incident.

The brightly lit bagel store was a welcome respite from holing up in a dark house with the prospect of existing on canned vegetables, tuna, and peanut butter crackers.

Peter counted six customers in line ahead of him. When it was his turn, he ordered seven containers of coffee and enough bagels and scrambled eggs to feed the three pajama party gals, Amy, Michael, and himself.

He made a quick stop at the front gate to drop off two coffees before he headed over to Emily's house to deliver the surprise breakfast. With the remaining food on the seat beside him, he imagined himself a caveman returning home to his family with a fresh kill slung over his shoulder.

Peter thought back to the middle of the night. He had finally dragged himself off to bed and was about to doze off when Amy tip-toed into his bedroom. At first, they cuddled and nuzzled each other's necks until he became fully erect. After a few delicious thrusts he couldn't hold back any longer. They climaxed together.

They rested in each other's arms for what felt like an eternity until Amy whispered, "I have to get back to Michael."

Peter ached for her to stay, but in that moment, he understood his world had shifted. The three of them would forever be a family now.

EIGHTY

PETER PUT HIS HANDS BEHIND his head and tilted his desk chair back as far back as it would go without toppling over. He relished these moments when he put his life in perspective and mentally categorized recent events under pros or cons.

Pro. Villa Paraiso survived Hurricane Arial with minimal damage.

Pro. There were no recent prowler sightings.

Pro. The landscaper had the recent Fig Whitefly infestation under control and saved hundreds of shrubs and trees.

Pro. Amy and his mother were getting along well, and Amy's son had proven to be a bonus. His mother had grown fond of the polite, well-behaved boy who, unlike Peter, performed well in school.

Pro. His mother announced she was moving to Villa Paraiso permanently, a definite two-for-one deal. Not only would she live nearby, but he would have one less villa in inventory.

Peter pulled one hand out from behind his head and counted, "One, two, three, four, five." Each time he recited a number, he held up another finger. "Five pros, no cons. Life is good."

His intercom buzzed. "Sorry I didn't give you a heads-up," Amy said. "Louis called earlier and insisted that I set up a three-way conference call before telling either you or Stu that he called."

Peter sat straight up in his chair. "What's up with him?"

"I thought it best not to ask questions," she said. "He sounded agitated and you know how nuts he can get."

Peter nodded. "And especially if he's juggling his head meds."

"What about the conference call?"

Peter braced himself. "Guess I have no choice. Put it through." He hit the speaker button.

"Peter, is that you?" Louis asked in a shaky voice.

"Yeah."

"I'm on the line, too," Stu said.

Silence on Louis' end.

Peter took a deep breath and said, "Amy said you have something important to tell us."

No response.

Peter drummed his fingers on the desk. "You've got a captive audience here, so what's on your mind?"

"Okay, okay," Louis said. "I just needed a minute to gather my thoughts. Here's the deal guys, and don't get me wrong, you've both been great. I can't imagine how I would've gotten my project off the ground without you, but well... something unexpected has come up and I need to move forward."

"Look, Louis," Peter said, "I don't know what you've been smoking or whose voice you hear in your head, but in case you haven't noticed we've been moving forward. Almost all the villas are sold and your so-called *project* is running like a well-oiled machine. I'm doing a bang-up job. What more do you want?"

"You'll get no argument from me," Louis said, "but..."

Peter shook his head. "Jesus, Louis, what the hell are you trying to say?"

"This isn't easy for me. I'm in a bind here, got involved with some bad dudes. You know me... one minute I'm up and the next minute I'm down. Well, this time I fell down the rabbit hole and landed in quicksand."

"What's that got to do with us?" Stu shouted on his end.

"These dudes I'm indebted to need to keep a close eye on me. They don't trust me."

"That comes as no surprise," Peter said, "but I'm with Stu. I don't see how it has anything to do with us."

"Well, actually it does. They want to bring in their own management team."

Peter exclaimed, "And you agreed to this?"

Silence.

"Say something, you little creep!"

"I had to, I had no choice."

"When is this moving forward taking place?" Peter asked.

"I told them I had to give you guys notice."

"How much notice?"

"Ninety days."

"That's it?" Peter said. "Ninety fuckin' days and we're history?"

"I'll try to hold them off a little longer, but it's in your contract, ninety days termination notice."

"It's a formality. Nobody takes that stuff seriously."

Stu screamed into the phone, "You're a loser! Always was and always will be. Never should've gotten mixed up with a screwed-up head-case like you."

"I don't deserve this abuse," Louis' voice cracked. "I'm not a bad person, ya' know."

"You're lucky you're not standing in front of me right now." Peter said. Heat rose from inside his collar. "You've said enough. Now shut up and crawl back into the hole you

289

came out of." He slammed down the phone and hunched over his desk, his hands curled into tightly balled fists.

Amy opened the office door, pointed to the phone and mouthed, "Stu's still holding."

"Shit. Tell him I'll get back to him later when I can think straight."

"You need to relax a little," she said. "Why don't you come to Chuck E. Cheese's with Michael and me after work tonight? I'm sure he'd love to see you."

"Sorry, kiddo, I'll be lousy company. I need some alone time. I've got a lot to think about." *A few minutes ago, I was counting my blessings and then, Louis... that crazy little prick turns my life upside-down.*

EIGHTY-ONE

PETER STUMBLED across plush carpeting and gazed through floor-to-ceiling windows in one of Stu's luxury rental properties. The rising sun shone like a gold medallion nestled in Mother Nature's bosom.

Stu had offered him the fully furnished penthouse free of charge. The high floor offered an unobstructed view that allowed Peter freedom to walk around naked with no one to see his protruding belly.

After a quick shower and a second cup of black coffee, Peter was ready to deal with the fallout from Louis' phone call. He grabbed the phone from the nightstand and punched in Stu's home phone number.

Stu answered his phone on the second ring. "Ordinarily, at this hour I'd reach through the phone and throttle the caller," Stu said, "but seeing as it's you I'll make an exception."

"You sound like I feel," Peter said.

"I didn't get one minute of sleep last night. How 'bout you?"

"The same." Peter shook his head. "I still can't get over the balls on that ungrateful weirdo bastard. And you... in all the years I've known you, I've never heard you get so angry."

"Angry? I wanted to rip his head off and shove it up his ass!"

"No sense in getting riled up again. There's really nothing we can do. We'll be more cautious next time."

"As far as I'm concerned, there's not going to be a next time."

"What now? For you it's business as usual. You're established down here. For me, it's different. I have to drag my ass back up north. And what do I do about Amy? I don't want to lose her."

"Hey buddy, we're a team. We go back a long way. We've looked out for each other since we were kids. Why don't you get your Florida Real Estate license? Should be a snap, you already have a New York license, don't you?"

"Yeah, but I still have to establish myself, work my way up. I dunno. I'm too old to start at the bottom."

"Who said anything about the bottom? You'll be working with your old buddy here."

"You make it sound like a slam-dunk."

"Believe me, it is," Stu said. "Oh, one more thing before I forget."

"What's that?"

"It's about time you find a permanent address. I bet Amy can help you with that."

"You dog, you."

"This change of plans may prove to be a blessing in disguise."

"How do you mean?" Peter asked.

"We won't have to deal with that head-case, Louis, anymore."

"Amen to that."

EIGHTY-TWO

THE SHERIFF'S OFFICE contacted Daniels regarding a Mexican illegal they'd been holding up in West Palm. An alert deputy linked the prisoner to the open murder case in South County. Eduardo had been arrested after a drunken brawl that left two Honduran brothers brutally beaten. During a disagreement over which South American soccer team would win the World Cup, he had threatened to chop them into fish food like he did to his redneck boss.

After a lengthy interrogation in which Eduardo was confronted with his mounting debt, confirmed by entries in Farley's notebook and the fish food reference, he broke down and confessed to Farley's murder.

* * *

Rosa stood at Amy's desk. "Manny told me to see Mr. Duke, *pronto*. Am I in trouble?"

"Not that I know of," Amy said. "Go right in." *That's one lucky lady*, Amy thought.

Rosa stood in Peter's open doorway and waited for him to look up.

"There she is," he said. "Come on in and have a seat."

She did as she was told.

"You're about to come into some money."

Her eyes opened wide.

"Remember Eduardo? He took off after the murder."

Rosa nodded.

"Well, it looks like the Sheriff's Office has him in custody, along with a signed confession. Trial oughta be a slam-dunk."

"I prayed for Farley's murderer to be caught," Rosa said. "I'm so happy. I can't wait to tell my sister, my friends." She leaped out of the chair and hugged Peter.

Her mind raced. First, she had to tell Hector the news. Then, she'd insist Maggie close the Café for one night to celebrate at an expensive restaurant with Hector and Manny. And after that, they'd be on their way to Walt Disney World.

* * *

At the end of the shift, Rosa waited for Hector with his time card clutched in her hand. She spotted him coming through the door and ran toward him.

"Hurry," she said, "punch out and meet me around back." Her feet barely touched the ground as she hurried outside.

A few seconds later, Hector came around the side of the building. "Whas up? You actin' *loca.*"

"You'd act *loca* too if you found out you're rich."

"Wha' you talkin' 'bout?"

"I'm rich. We're rich, you and me!"

"You scarin' me."

Rosa bubbled with excitement as she recounted her visit to Peter's office. She waited for Hector's reaction. "Now *you're* scaring me," she said after a long silence.

"Don' know what you wan' me to say."

Rosa placed her hand on his arm. "You can say, 'congratulations'. You can say, 'I love you'."

Hector's pulse quickened. His breathing became labored, followed by a dull pain in the center of his chest. *I can no be the man she wan' me to be. She deserve a man with pure heart and mind.* He pulled his arm away. "I mus' go."

Rosa let out a loud sigh as she watched Hector flee once again. *I have shed my last tears for you, Hector Valezquez. Adios, mi amor. I will never forget you.*

EIGHTY-THREE

A CANADIAN COLD FRONT drifted along the east coast before it settled over South Florida. Powerful winds and torrential rains alternated with glorious days of unabated sunshine.

Hector awoke to the sound of rolling thunder accompanied by slashes of blinding lightning. He threw back his rumpled bed sheet. Cool air washed over his naked body. A freight train's whistle wailed in the distance, followed by silence, the night as still as he imagined death to be.

He winced as lightning cracked and thunder boomed. His mood darkened. He was tired of lying to everyone, but most of all, he was tired of lying to himself. He could no longer deny the painful truth. Peering into windows excited him and relieved his sexual urges.

He covered his eyes with the palms of his hands. *No one can help me... Dr. Bennett... Rosa... no one.*

He reached up, pulled the overhead light chain, and surveyed his tiny room, a replica of other squalid places he had lived in after he left home. The smell of mildew and rust burned his nostrils.

He dressed in haste and stuffed his meager possessions into a duffle bag, turned off the light, and groped his way through the darkened house until he reached the front door. With his hand resting on the doorknob, Hector hesitated for a moment before he slipped into the cool dense fog and disappeared into the mist.

* * *

The rising sun outlines the wafer-thin stratus clouds framed by gold and yellow ribbons. A magnificent tapestry floats effortlessly across the sky as an egret swoops low and settles atop a hibiscus tree. Vibrant royal poinciana blossoms are ablaze in brilliant sunlight. Villa Paraiso residents' laughter and tears, declarations of love and fidelity, illicit romances, secrets and lies ebb and flow with each new day... each exquisite new day in Paradise.

ACKNOWLEDGMENTS

FOR YOUR WORDS of encouragement and your input, my thanks to:

- my loving family and friends,
- Mindy and Rich Elkins, Michael Breit, Kathy M. Runk, Alexandra Goodwin, Mari Mitchell, Trey McIntosh and Kathy Velasco,
- Ben Adler, Ph.D.,
- the multitalented A.R. Allen, Lea Becker, Col. Joe Beradino, Bea Lewis, Michelle Putnik, Linda Rosen, Bunny Shulman, Charlie Sterbakov, Carren Strock and Pat Williams,
- FWA's Caryn DeVincenti and her equally talented writing group,
- my editor, Shirley Carrie-Hartman,
- my publisher, Penelope Love, and cover designer, Rolf Busch, at Citrine Publishing, and
- photographer William Bracht for the back cover photo.

ABOUT THE AUTHOR

LEE B. RAVINE holds a Bachelor of Arts in Psychology and a Master of Science in Special Education.

She began her career as a paraprofessional with the New York City public school system and went on to teach her beloved special needs students. After moving to Florida, Lee volunteered as a domestic violence victims' advocate with the Palm Beach County Sheriff's Office. She continues her volunteer work with the Faulk Center for Counseling.

Lee is the author of *Riding Solo My Journey Through Love And Madness.*

When she isn't working on her new novel exposing more secrets and lies, Lee is available as a guest speaker. She offers entertaining and informative programs.

For more information:
Call (561) 470-1580
Email: profLBR@aol.com
Visit www.leeravine.com